William B. Yeats

John Sherman and Dhoya

William B. Yeats

John Sherman and Dhoya

ISBN/EAN: 9783337400439

Printed in Europe, USA, Canada, Australia, Japan

Cover: Foto ©Andreas Hilbeck / pixelio.de

More available books at **www.hansebooks.com**

GANCONAGH

JOHN SHERMAN

AND

DHOYA

SECOND EDITION

LONDON
T. FISHER UNWIN
PATERNOSTER SQUARE
—
M DCCC XCI

GANCONAGH'S APOLOGY.

HE maker of these stories has been told that he must not bring them to you himself. He has asked me to pretend that I am the author. I am an old little Irish spirit, and I sit in the hedges and watch the world go by. I see the boys going to market driving donkeys with creels of turf, and the girls carrying baskets of apples. Sometimes I call to some pretty face, and we chat a little in the shadow, the apple basket before us, for, as my faithful historian O'Kearney has put it in his now yellow manuscript, I care for nothing in the world but love and idleness. Will not

you, too, sit down under the shade of the bushes while I read you the stories ? The first I do not care for because it deals with dull persons and the world's affairs, but the second has to do with my own people. If my voice at whiles grows distant and dreamy when I talk of the world's affairs, remember that I have seen all from my hole in the hedge. I hear continually the songs of my own people who dance upon the hill-side, and am content. I have never carried apples or driven turf myself, or if I did it was only in a dream. Nor do my kind use any of man's belongings except the little black pipes which the farmers find now and then when they are turning the sods over with a plough.

GANCONAGH.

PART I.

JOHN SHERMAN LEAVES BALLAH.

I.

ON the west of Ireland, on the 9th of December, in the town of Ballah, in the Imperial Hotel there was a single guest, clerical and youthful. With the exception of a stray commercial traveller, who stopped once for a night, there had been nobody for a whole month but this guest, and now he was thinking of going away. The town, full enough in summer of trout and salmon fishers, slept all winter like the bears.

On the evening of the 9th of December, in the coffee-room of the Imperial Hotel, there was nobody but this guest. The guest was irritated. It had rained all day, and now that it was clearing up night had almost fallen. He had packed his portmanteau: his stockings, his clothes-brush, his razor, his dress shoes were each in their corner, and now he had nothing to do. He had tried the paper that was lying on the table. He did not agree with its politics.

The waiter was playing an accordion in a little room over the stairs. The guest's irritation increased, for the more he thought about it the more he perceived that the accordion was badly played. There was a piano in the coffee-room; he sat down at it and played the tune correctly, as loudly as possible. The waiter took no notice. He did not know that he was being played for. He was wholly absorbed in his own playing, and besides he was old, obstinate, and deaf. The guest could stand it no longer. He rang for the waiter, and then, remembering that he did not need anything, went out before he came.

He went through Martin's
Street, and Peter's Lane, and
turned down by the burnt house
at the corner of the fish-market,
picking his way towards the
bridge. The town was dripping,
but the rain was almost over.
The large drops fell seldomer and
seldomer into the puddles. It
was the hour of ducks. Three
or four had squeezed themselves
under a gate, and were now
splashing about in the gutter of
the main street. There was
scarcely any one abroad. Once
or twice a countryman went by in
yellow gaiters covered with mud
and looked at the guest. Once
an old woman with a basket of
clothes, recognizing the Protestant curate's *locum tenens*, made a
low curtsey.

The clouds gradually drifted
away, the twilight deepened and
the stars came out. The guest,
having bought some cigarettes,
had spread his waterproof on the
parapet of the bridge and was
now leaning his elbows upon it,

looking at the river and feeling
at last quite tranquil. His
meditations, he repeated, to
himself, were plated with
silver by the stars. The water
slid noiselessly, and one or
two of the larger stars made
little roadways of fire into the
darkness. The light from a distant casement made also its
roadway. Once or twice a fish
leaped. Along the banks were
the vague shadows of houses,
seeming like phantoms gathering
to drink.

Yes; he felt now quite contented with the world. Amidst
his enjoyment of the shadows and
the river—a veritable festival of
silence—was mixed pleasantly the
knowledge that, as he leant there
with the light of a neighbouring
gas-jet, flickering faintly on his
refined form and nervous face
and glancing from the little medal
of some Anglican order that
hung upon his watch-guard, he
must have seemed—if there had
been any to witness—a being

of a different kind to the
inhabitants—at once rough and
conventional — of this half-
deserted town. Between these
two feelings the unworldly and
the worldly tossed a leaping wave
of perfect enjoyment. How
pleasantly conscious of his own
identity it made him when he
thought how he and not those
whose birthright it was, felt
most the beauty of these shadows
and this river? To him who had
read much, seen operas and
plays, known religious experi-
ences, and written verse to a
waterfall in Switzerland, and not
to those who dwelt upon its bor-
ders for their whole lives, did this
river raise a tumult of images and
wonders. What meaning it had for
them he could not imagine. Some
meaning surely it must have!

As he gazed out into the
darkness, spinning a web of
thoughts from himself to the
river, from the river to himself,
he saw, with a corner of his eye,
a spot of red light moving in the

air at the other end of the bridge.
He turned towards it. It came
closer and closer, there ap-
pearing behind it the while a
man and a cigar. The man
carried in one hand a mass of
fishing-line covered with hooks,
and in the other a tin porringer
full of bait.

" Good evening, Howard."

" Good evening," answered the
guest, taking his elbows off the
parapet and looking in a preoccupied way at the man with the
hooks. It was only gradually
he remembered that he was in
Ballah among the barbarians,
for his mind had strayed from
the last evening gnats, making
circles on the water beneath, to
the devil's song against " the
little spirits " in " Mefistofele."
Looking down at the stone
parapet he considered a moment
and then burst out—

" Sherman, how do you stand
this place — you who have
thoughts above mere eating and
sleeping and are not always grind-

ing at the stubble mill?   Here
everybody lives in the eighteenth
century—the   squalid   century.
Well, I am going to-morrow,
you know.   Thank   Heaven, I
am done with your grey streets
and grey minds!   The curate
must come home, sick or well.
I have a religious   essay to
write, and besides I should
die.   Think   of   that old fellow
at the corner there, our most
important parishioner.   There
are no more hairs on his head
than thoughts in his skull.   To
merely look at him is to rob
life of its dignity.   Then there is
nothing in the shops but school-
books and Sunday-school prizes.
Excellent, no doubt, for any one
who has not had to read as many
as I have.   Such a choir! such
rain!"

"You need some occupation
peculiar to the place," said the
other, baiting his hooks with
worms out of the little porringer.
"I catch eels.   You should set
some night-lines too.   You bait

them with worms in this way,
and put them among the weeds
at the edge of the river. In the
morning you find an eel or two, if
you have good fortune, turning
round and round and making the
weeds sway. I shall catch a
great many after this rain."

"What a suggestion! Do you
mean to stay here," said Howard,
"till your mind rots like our
most important parishioner's?"

"No, no! To be quite frank
with you," replied the other, " I
have some good looks and shall
try to turn them to account by
going away from here pretty soon
and trying to persuade some girl
with money to fall in love with
me. I shall not be altogether a
bad match, you see, because after
she has made me a little prosperous my uncle will die and
make me much more so. I wish
to be able always to remain a
lounger. Yes, I shall marry
money. My mother has set her
heart on it, and I am not, you
see, the kind of person who falls

in love inconveniently.   For the
present——"

"You are vegetating," interrupted the other.

"No, I am seeing the world.
In your big towns a man finds ʹ
his minority and knows nothing ⁻
outside its border.   He knows
only the people like himself.
But here one chats with the
whole world in a day's walk, for
every man one meets is a class.
The knowledge I am picking up
may be useful to me when I enter
the great cities and their ignor-
ance.   But I have lines to set.
Come with me.   I would ask
you home, but you and my
mother, you know, do not get
on well."

"I could not live with any
one I did not believe in," said
Howard; "you are so different
from me.   You can live with
mere facts, and that is why, I
suppose, your schemes are so
mercenary.   Before this beautiful
river, these stars, these great
purple shadows, do you not feel

like an insect in a flower? As for
me, I also have planned my
future. Not too near or too far
from a great city I see myself in
a cottage with diamond panes,
sitting by the fire. There are
books everywhere and etchings
on the wall; on the table is a
manuscript essay on some religious matter. Perhaps I shall
marry some day. Probably not,
for I shall ask so much. Certainly I shall not marry for
money, for I hold the directness
and sincerity of the nature to be
its compass. If we once break
it the world grows trackless."

"Good-bye," said Sherman,
briskly; "I have baited the last
hook. Your schemes suit you,
but a sluggish fellow like me,
poor devil, who wishes to lounge
through the world, would find
them expensive."

They parted; Sherman to set
his lines and Howard to his
hotel in high spirits, for it seemed
to him he had been eloquent.
The billiard-room, which opened

on the street, was lighted up. A
few young men came round to
play sometimes. He went in,
for among these provincial youths
he felt *recherché;* besides, he was a
really good player. As he came
in one of the players missed and
swore. Howard reproved him
with a look. He joined the play
for a time, and then catching
sight through a distant door of
the hotel-keeper's wife putting a
kettle on the hob he hurried off,
and, drawing a chair to the fire,
began one of those long gossips
about everybody's affairs peculiar
to the cloth.

As Sherman, having set his
lines, returned home, he passed a
tobacconist's—a sweet-shop and
tobacconist's in one—the only
shop in town, except public-
houses, that remained open. The
tobacconist was standing in his
door, and, recognizing one who
dealt consistently with a rival
at the other end of the town,
muttered : " There goes that
gluggerabunthaun and Jack o'

Dreams; been fishing most
likely. Ugh!" Sherman paused
for a moment as he repassed the
bridge and looked at the water,
on which now a new-risen and
crescent moon was shining dimly.
How full of memories it was to
him ! what playmates and boyish
adventures did it not bring to
mind! To him it seemed to say,
" Stay near to me," as to Howard
it had said, " Go yonder, to those
other joys and other sceneries I
have told you of." It bade him
who loved stay still and dream,
and gave flying feet to him who
imagined.

II.

THE house where Sherman and his mother lived was one of those bare houses so common in country towns. Their dashed fronts mounting above empty pavements have a kind of dignity in their utilitarianism. They seem to say, "Fashion has not made us, nor ever do its caprices pass our sand-cleaned doorsteps." On every basement window is the same dingy wire blind; on every door the same brass knocker. Custom everywhere ! "So much the longer," the blinds seem to say, "have eyes glanced through us"; and the knockers to murmur, "And fingers lifted us."

No. 15, Stephens' Row, was in
no manner peculiar among its
twenty fellows. The chairs in
the drawing-room facing the
street were of heavy mahogany
with horsehair cushions worn at
the corners. On the round table
was somebody's commentary on
the New Testament laid like the
spokes of a wheel on a table-
cover of American oilcloth with
stamped Japanese figures half
worn away. The room was seldom used, for Mrs. Sherman was
solitary because silent. In this
room the dressmaker sat twice a
year, and here the rector's wife
used every month or so to drink
a cup of tea. It was quite clean.
There was not a fly-mark on the
mirror, and all summer the fern
in the grate was constantly
changed. Behind this room and
overlooking the garden was the
parlour, where cane-bottomed
chairs took the place of mahogany. Sherman had lived here
with his mother all his life, and
their old servant hardly remem-

bered having lived anywhere else; and soon she would absolutely cease to remember the world she knew before she saw the four walls of this house, for every day she forgot something fresh. The son was almost thirty, the mother fifty, and the servant near seventy. Every year they had two hundred pounds among them, and once a year the son got a new suit of clothes and went into the drawing-room to look at himself in the mirror.

On the morning of the 20th of December Mrs. Sherman was down before her son. A spare, delicate-featured woman, with somewhat thin lips tightly closed as with silent people, and eyes at once gentle and distrustful, tempering the hardness of the lips. She helped the servant to set the table, and then, for her old-fashioned ideas would not allow her to rest, began to knit, often interrupting her knitting to go into the kitchen or to listen at the foot of the stairs. At last, hearing a sound upstairs, she put the eggs down to boil, muttering the while, and began again to knit. When her son appeared she received him with a smile.

"Late again, mother," he said.

" The young should sleep," she answered, for to her he seemed still a boy.

She had finished her breakfast some time before the young man, and because it would have appeared very wrong to her to leave the table, she sat on knitting behind the tea-urn : an industry the benefit of which was felt by many poor children—almost the only neighbours she had a good word for.

" Mother," said the young man, presently, " your friend the *locum tenens* is off to-morrow."

" A good riddance."

" Why are you so hard on him ? He talked intelligently when here, I thought," answered her son.

" I do not like his theology,"

she replied, "nor his way of running about and flirting with this body and that body, nor his way of chattering while he buttons and unbuttons his gloves."

"You forget he is a man of the great world, and has about him a manner that must seem strange to us."

"Oh, he might do very well," she answered, "for one of those Carton girls at the rectory."

"That eldest girl is a good girl," replied her son.

"She looks down on us all, and thinks herself intellectual," she went on. "I remember when girls were content with their Catechism and their Bibles and a little practice at the piano, maybe, for an accomplishment. What does any one want more? It is all pride."

"You used to like her as a child," said the young man.

"I like all children."

Sherman having finished his breakfast, took a book of travels in one hand and a trowel in the

other and went out into the garden.
Having looked under the parlour
window for the first tulip shoots,
he went down to the further end
and began covering some sea-kale
for forcing. He had not been
long at work when the servant
brought him a letter. There was
a stone roller at one side of the
grass plot. He sat down upon it,
and taking the letter between his
finger and thumb began looking
at it with an air that said:
" Well! I know what you
mean." He remained long thus
without opening it, the book
lying beside him on the roller.

The garden—the letter—the
book! You have there the three
symbols of his life. Every
morning he worked in that
garden among the sights and
sounds of nature. Month by
month he planted and hoed and
dug there. In the middle he had
set a hedge that divided the
garden in two. Above the hedge
were flowers; below it, vegetables. At the furthest end from

the house, lapping broken
masonry full of wallflowers, the
river said, month after month to
all upon its banks, " Hush ! "
He dined at two with perfect
regularity, and in the afternoon
went out to shoot or walk.
At twilight he set night-lines.
Later on he read. He had not
many books — a Shakespeare,
Mungo Park's travels, a few
two-shilling novels, " Percy's
Reliques," and a volume on
etiquette. He seldom varied his
occupations. He had no pro-
fession. The town talked of it.
They said : " He lives upon his
mother," and were very angry.
They never let him see this,
however, for it was generally
understood he would be a
dangerous fellow to rouse ; but
there was an uncle from whom
Sherman had expectations who
sometimes wrote remonstrating.
Mrs. Sherman resented these
letters, for she was afraid of her
son going away to seek his fortune—perhaps even in America.

Now this matter preyed somewhat on Sherman.   For three
years or so he had been trying to
make his mind up and come to
some decision. Sometimes when
reading he would start and press
his lips together and knit his
brows for a moment.

It will now be seen why the
garden, the book, and the letter
were the three symbols of his
life, summing up as they did his
love of out-of-door doings, his
meditations, his anxieties.   His
life in the garden had granted
serenity to his forehead, the
reading of his few books had
filled his eyes with reverie, and
the feeling that he was not quite
a good citizen had given a slight
and occasional trembling to his
lips.

He opened the letter.   Its
contents were what he had long
expected. His uncle offered to
take him into his office.   He laid
it spread out before him—a foot
on each margin, right and left—
and looked at it, turning the

matter over and over in his mind.
Would he go? would he stay?
He did not like the idea much.
The lounger in him did not
enjoy the thought of London.
Gradually his mind wandered
away into scheming — infinite
scheming—what he would do if
he went, what he would do if he
did not go.

A beetle, attracted by the faint
sunlight, had crawled out of his
hole. It saw the paper and
crept on to it, the better to catch
the sunlight. Sherman saw the
beetle but his mind was not
occupied with it. " Shall I tell
Mary Carton ? " he was thinking.
Mary had long been his adviser
and friend. She was, indeed,
everybody's adviser. Yes, he
would ask her what to do.
Then again he thought—no, he
would decide for himself. The
beetle began to move. " If it
goes off the paper by the top I
will ask her—if by the bottom I
will not."

The beetle went off by the

3

top. He got up with an air of
decision and went into the tool-
house and began sorting seeds
and picking out the light ones,
sometimes stopping to watch a
spider; for he knew he must wait
till the afternoon to see Mary
Carton. The tool-house was a
favourite place with him. He
often read there and watched the
spiders in the corners.

At dinner he was preoccupied.

" Mother," he said, " would
you much mind if we went away
from this ? "

" I have often told you," she
answered, " I do not like one
place better than another. I
like them all equally little."

After dinner he went again
into the tool-house. This time
he did not sort seeds—only
watched the spiders.

III.

TOWARDS evening he went out. The pale sunshine of winter flickered on his path. The wind blew the straws about. He grew more and more melancholy. A dog of his acquaintance was chasing rabbits in a field. He had never been known to catch one, and since his youth had never seen one for he was almost wholly blind. They were his form of the eternal chimera. The dog left the field and followed with a friendly sniff.

They came together to the rectory. Mary Carton was not in. There was a children's practice in the school-house. They went thither.

A child of four or five with a

swelling on its face was sitting
under a wall opposite the school
door, waiting to make faces at
the Protestant children as they
came out.   Catching sight of
the dog she seemed to debate in
her mind whether to throw a
stone at it or call it to her.
She threw the stone and made
it run.   In after times he remembered all these things as
though they were of importance.

He opened the latched green
door and went in.   About twenty
children were singing in shrill
voices standing in a row at the
further end.   At the harmonium
he recognized Mary Carton, who
nodded to him and went on with
her playing.   The white-washed
walls were covered with glazed
prints of animals; at the further
end was a large map of Europe;
by a fire at the near end was a
table with the remains of tea.
This tea was an idea of Mary's.
They had tea and cake first,
afterwards the singing.   The
floor was covered with crumbs.

The fire was burning brightly. Sherman sat down beside it. A child with a great deal of oil in her hair was sitting on the end of a form at the other side.

"Look," she whispered, "I have been sent away. At any rate they are further from the fire. They have to be near the harmonium. I would not sing. Do you like hymns? I don't. Will you have a cup of tea? I can make it quite well. See, I did not spill a drop. Have you enough milk?" It was a cup full of milk—children's tea. "Look, there is a mouse carrying away a crumb. Hush!"

They sat there, the child watching the mouse, Sherman pondering on his letter, until the music ceased and the children came tramping down the room. The mouse having fled, Sherman's self-appointed hostess got up with a sigh and went out with the others.

Mary Carton closed the harmonium and came towards

Sherman. Her face and all her movements showed a gentle decision of character. Her glance was serene, her features regular, her figure at the same time ample and beautifully moulded; her dress plain yet not without a certain air of distinction. In a different society she would have had many suitors. But she was of a type that in country towns does not get married at all. Its beauty is too lacking in pink and white, its nature in that small assertiveness admired for character by the uninstructed. Elsewhere she would have known her own beauty—as it is right that all the beautiful should—and have learnt how to display it, to add gesture to her calm and more of mirth and smiles to her grave cheerfulness. As it was, her manner was much older than herself.

She sat down by Sherman with the air of an old friend. They had long been accustomed to consult together on every matter. They were such good friends they had never fallen in love with each other. Perfect love and perfect friendship are indeed incompatible; for the one is a battlefield where shadows war beside the combatants, and the other a placid country where Consultation has her dwelling.

These two were such good friends that the most gossiping townspeople had given them up with a sigh. The doctor's wife, a faded beauty and devoted romance reader, said one day, as they passed, "They are such cold creatures." The old maid who kept the Berlin-wool shop remarked, "They are not of the marrying sort," and now their comings and goings were no longer noticed. Nothing had ever come to break in on their quiet companionship and give obscurity as a dwelling-place for the needed illusions. Had one been weak and the other strong, one plain and the other handsome, one guide and the other guided, one wise and the other foolish, love might have found them out in a moment, for love is based on inequality as friendship is on equality.

"John," said Mary Carton, warming her hands at the fire, "I have had a troublesome day. Did you come to help me teach the children to sing ? It was good of you : you were just too late."

"No," he answered, "I have come to be your pupil. I am always your pupil."

"Yes, and a most disobedient one."

"Well, advise me this time at any rate. My uncle has written, offering me £100 a year to begin with in his London office. Am I to go ? "

"You – know quite well my answer," she said.

"Indeed I do not. Why should I go ? I am contented here. I am now making my garden ready for spring. Later on there will be trout fishing

and saunters by the edge of the
river in the evening when the
bats are flickering about. In
July there will be races. I
enjoy the bustle. I enjoy life
here. When anything annoys
me I keep away from it, that
is all. You know I am always
busy. I have occupation and
friends and am quite contented."

"It is a great loss to many of
us, but you must go, John," she
said. "For you know you will
be old some day, and perhaps
when the vitality of youth is
gone you will feel that your life
is empty and find that you are
too old to change it ; and you
will give up, perhaps, trying to
be happy and likeable and
become as the rest are. I think
I can see you," she said, with a
laugh, "a hypochondriac, like
Gorman, the retired excise
officer, or with a red nose like
Dr. Stephens, or growing like
Peters, the elderly cattle mer-
chant, who starves his horse."

"They were bad material to

begin with," he answered, "and besides, I cannot take my mother away with me at her age, and I cannot leave her alone."

"What annoyance it may be," she answered, "will soon be forgotten. You will be able to give her many more comforts. We women—we all like to be dressed well and have pleasant rooms to sit in, and a young man at your age should not be idle. You must go away from this little backward place. We shall miss you, but you are clever and must go and work with other men and have your talents admitted."

"How emulous you would have me. Perhaps I shall be well-to-do some day; meanwhile I only wish to stay here with my friends."

She went over to the window and looked out with her face turned from him. The evening light cast a long shadow behind her on the floor. After some moments, she said, "I see

people ploughing on the slope
of the hill. There are people
working on a house to the right.
Everywhere there are people
busy," and, with a slight tremble
in her voice, she added, " and,
John, nowhere are there any
doing what they wish. One has
to think of so many things—of
duty and God."

" Mary, I didn't know you
were so religious."

Coming towards him with a
smile, she said, " No more did
I, perhaps. But sometimes the
self in one is very strong. One
has to think a great deal and
reason with it. Yet I try hard
to lose myself in things about
me. These children now — I
often lie awake thinking about
them. That child who was
talking to you is often on my
mind. I do not know what will
happen to her. She makes me
unhappy. I am afraid she is
not a good child at all. I am
afraid she is not taught well at
home. I try hard to be gentle

and patient with her. I am a
little displeased with myself to-
day; so I have lectured you.
There! I have made my confession. But," she added, taking one of his hands in both
hers and reddening, "you must
go away. You must not be idle.
You will gain everything."

As she stood there with bright
eyes, the light of evening about
her, Sherman for perhaps the
first time saw how beautiful she
was, and was flattered by her
interest. For the first time also
her presence did not make him
at peace with the world.

"Will you be an obedient
pupil?"

"You know so much more than
I do," he answered, "and are
so much wiser. I will write to
my uncle and agree to his offer."

"Now you must go home,"
she said. "You must not keep
your mother waiting for her tea.
There! I have raked the fire
out. We must not forget to
lock the door behind us."

As they stood on the doorstep the wind blew a whirl of dead leaves about them.

" They are my old thoughts," he said; " see, they are all withered."

They walked together silently. At the vicarage he left her and went homeward.

The deserted flour store at the corner of two roads, the house that had been burnt hollow ten years before and still lifted its blackened beams, the straggling and leafless fruit-trees rising above garden walls, the church where he was christened—these foster-mothers of his infancy seemed to nod and shake their heads over him.

" Mother," he said, hurriedly entering the room, " we are going to London."

" As you wish. I always knew you would be a rolling stone," she answered, and went out to tell the servant that as soon as she had finished the week's washing they must pack up everything, for they were going to London.

" Yes, we must pack up," said the old peasant; she did not stop peeling the onion in her hand — she had not comprehended. In the middle of the night she suddenly started up in bed with a pale face and a prayer to the Virgin whose image hung over her head — she had now comprehended.

IV.

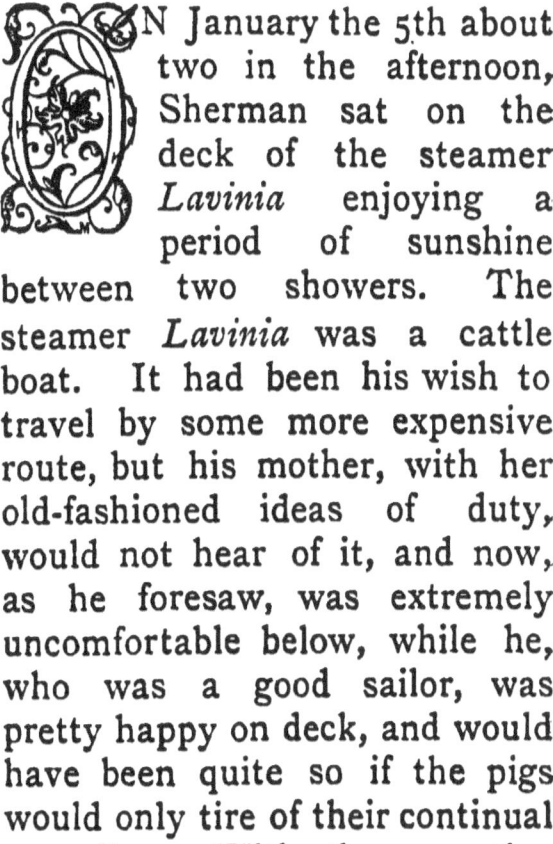N January the 5th about two in the afternoon, Sherman sat on the deck of the steamer *Lavinia* enjoying a period of sunshine between two showers. The steamer *Lavinia* was a cattle boat. It had been his wish to travel by some more expensive route, but his mother, with her old-fashioned ideas of duty, would not hear of it, and now, as he foresaw, was extremely uncomfortable below, while he, who was a good sailor, was pretty happy on deck, and would have been quite so if the pigs would only tire of their continual squealing. With the exception

of a very dirty old woman sitting by a crate of geese, all the passengers but himself were below. This old woman made the journey monthly with geese for the Liverpool market.

Sherman was dreaming. He began to feel very desolate, and commenced a letter to Mary Carton in his notebook to state this fact. He was a laborious and unpractised writer, and found it helped him to make a pencil copy. Sometimes he stopped and watched the puffin sleeping on the waves. Each one of them had its head tucked in in a somewhat different way. That is because their characters are different," he thought.

Gradually he began to notice a great many corks floating by, one after the other. The old woman saw them too, and said, waking out of a half sleep—

" Misther John Sherman, we will be in the Mersey before evening. Why are ye goin' among them savages in London,

Misther John? Why don't ye
stay among your own people—
for what have we in this life but
a mouthful of air?"

PART II.

MARGARET LELAND.

I.

SHERMAN and his mother rented a small house on the north side of St. Peter's Square, Hammersmith. The front windows looked out on to the old rank and green square, the windows behind on to a little patch of garden round which the houses gathered and pressed as though they already longed to trample it out. In this garden was a single tall pear-tree that never bore fruit.

Three years passed by without any notable event. Sherman went every day to his office in Tower Hill Street, abused his work a great deal, and was not unhappy perhaps. He was probably a bad clerk, but then nobody was very exacting with the nephew of the head of the firm.

The firm of Sherman and Saunders, ship brokers, was a long-established, old-fashioned house. Saunders had been dead some years and old Michael Sherman ruled alone — an old bachelor full of family pride and pride in his wealth. He lived, for all that, in a very simple fashion. His mahogany furniture was a little solider than other people's perhaps. He did not understand display. Display finds its excuse in some taste good or bad, and in a long industrious life Michael Sherman had never found leisure to form one. He seemed to live only from habit. Year by year he grew more silent, gradually ceasing to regard anything but his family and his ships. His family were represented by his nephew and his nephew's mother. He did not feel much affection for them. He believed in his family—that

'as all. To remind him of the
ther goal of his thoughts hung
ɔund his private office pictures
ɿith such inscriptions as " S.S.
ndus at the Cape of Good
Iope," " The barque *Mary* in
he Mozambique Channel," "The
arque *Livingstone* at Port Said,"
nd many more. Every rope was
rawn accurately with a ruler,
nd here and there were added
istant vessels sailing proudly
ɿy with all that indifference to
ɿerspective peculiar to the draw-
ngs of sailors. On every ship
ɿas the flag of the firm spread
ɿut to show the letters.

No man cared for old Michael
Sherman. Every one liked John.
3oth were silent, but the young
nan had sometimes a talkative
it. The old man lived for his
edger, the young man for his
lreams.

In spite of all these differences,
the uncle was on the whole
pleased with the nephew. He
noticed a certain stolidity that
was of the family. It sometimes

irritated others.   It pleased him.
He saw a hundred indications
besides that made him say, " He
is a true Sherman.   We Shermans begin that way and give
up frivolity as we grow old.   We
are all the same in the end."

Mrs. Sherman and her son
had but a small round of
acquaintances — a few rich
people, clients of the house of
Sherman and Saunders for the
most part.   Among these was a
Miss Margaret Leland who lived
with her mother, the widow of
the late Henry Leland, ship-
broker, on the eastern side of St.
Peter's Square.   Their house
was larger than the Shermans,
and noticeable among its fellows
by the newly-painted hall door.
Within on every side were
bronzes and china vases and
heavy curtains.   In all were dis-
played the curious and vagrant
taste of Margaret Leland.   The
rich   Italian   and   mediæval
draperies of the pre-Raphaelites

jostling the brightest and vulgarest products of more native and Saxon schools. Vases of the most artistic shape and colour side by side with artificial flowers and stuffed birds. This house belonged to the Lelands. They had bought it in less prosperous days, and having altered it according to their taste and the need of their growing welfare could not decide to leave it.

Sherman was an occasional caller at the Lelands, and had certainly a liking, though not a very deep one, for Margaret. As yet he knew little more about her than that she wore the most fascinating hats, that the late Lord Lytton was her favourite author, and that she hated frogs. It is clear that she did not know that a French writer on magic says the luxurious and extravagant hate frogs because they are cold, solitary, and dreary. Had she done so, she would have been more circumspect about revealing her tastes.

4

For the rest John Sherman
was forgetting the town of
Ballah. He corresponded indeed
with Mary Carton, but his laborious letter writing made his
letters fewer and fewer. Sometimes, too, he heard from
Howard, who had a curacy in
Glasgow and was on indifferent
terms with his parishioners.
They objected to his way of
conducting the services. His
letters were full of it. He would
not give in, he said, whatever
happened. His conscience was
involved.

II.

NE afternoon Mrs. Leland called on Mrs. Sherman. She very often called — this fat, sentimental woman, moving in the midst of a cloud of scent. The day was warm, and she carried her too elaborate and heavy dress as a large caddis-fly drags its case with much labour and patience. She sat down on the sofa with obvious relief, leaning so heavily among the cushions that a clothes-moth in an antimacassar thought the end of the world had come and fluttered out only to be knocked down and crushed by Mrs. Sherman, who was very quick in her movements.

As soon as she found her breath, Mrs. Leland began a long history of her sorrows. Her daughter Margaret, had been jilted and was in despair, had taken to her bed with every resolution to die, and was grow-ing paler and paler. The hard-hearted man, though she knew he had heard, did not relent. She knew he had heard because her daughter had told his sister all about it, and his sister had no heart, because she said it was temper that ailed Margaret, and she was a little vixen, and that if she had not flirted with everybody the engagement would never have been broken off. But Mr. Sims had no heart clearly, as Miss Marriot and Mrs. Eliza Taylor, her daughter's friends, said, when they heard, and Lock, the butler, said the same too, and Mary Young, the house-maid, said so too—and she knew all about it, for Margaret used to read his letters to her often when having her hair brushed.

"She must have been very fond of him," said Mrs. Sherman.

"She is so romantic, my dear," answered Mrs. Leland, with a sigh. "I am afraid she takes after an uncle on her father's side, who wrote poetry and wore a velvet jacket and ran away with an Italian countess who used to get drunk. When I married Mr. Leland people said he was not worthy of me, and that I was throwing myself away—and he in business, too! But Margaret is so romantic. There was Mr. Walters, the gentleman farmer, and Simpson who had a jeweller's shop—I never approved of him!—and Mr. Samuelson, and the Hon. William Scott. She tired of them all except the Hon. William Scott, who tired of her because some one told him she put belladonna in her eyes—and it is not true ; and now there is Mr. Sims!" She then cried a little, and allowed herself to be consoled by Mrs. Sherman.

"You talk so intelligently and

are so well informed," she said at parting. "I have made a very pleasant call," and the caddis-worm toiled upon its way, arriving in due course at other cups of tea.

III.

HE day after Mrs. Leland's call upon his mother, John Sherman, returning home after his not very lengthy day in the office, saw Margaret coming towards him. She had a lawn tennis racket under her arm, and was walking slowly on the shady side of the road. She was a pretty girl with quite irregular features, who though really not more than pretty, had so much manner, so much of an air, that every one called her a beauty: a trefoil with the fragrance of a rose.

"Mr. Sherman," she cried, coming smiling to meet him, "I

have been ill, but could not stand
the house any longer. I am going
to the Square to play tennis.
Will you come with me?"

"I am a bad player," he said.

"Of course you are," she answered; "but you are the only
person under a hundred to be
found this afternoon. How dull
life is!" she continued, with a
sigh. "You heard how ill I have
been? What do you do all
day?"

"I sit at a desk, sometimes
writing, and sometimes, when I
get lazy, looking up at the flies.
There are fourteen on the plaster
of the ceiling over my head.
They died two winters ago. I
sometimes think to have them
brushed off, but they have been
there so long now I hardly like
to."

"Ah! you like them," she
said, "because you are accustomed to them. In most
cases there is not much more
to be said for our family affections, I think."

"In a room close at hand," he went on, "there is, you know, Uncle Michael, who never speaks."

"Precisely. You have an uncle who never speaks; I have a mother who never is silent. She went to see Mrs. Sherman the other day. What did she say to her?"

"Nothing."

"Really. What a dull thing existence is!"—this with a great sigh. "When the Fates are weaving our web of life some mischievous goblin always runs off with the dye-pot. Everything is dull and grey. Am I looking a little pale? I have been so very ill."

"A little bit pale, perhaps," he said, doubtfully.

The Square gate brought them to a stop. It was locked, but she had the key. The lock was stiff, but turned easily for John Sherman.

"How strong you are," she said.

It was an iridescent evening
of spring. The leaves of the
bushes had still their faint
green. As Margaret darted
about at the tennis, a red
feather in her cap seemed to
rejoice with its wearer. Everything was at once gay and tranquil. The whole world had that
unreal air it assumes at beautiful
moments, as though it might
vanish at a touch like an iridescent soap-bubble.

After a little Margaret said
she was tired, and, sitting on a
garden seat among the bushes,
began telling him the plots of
novels lately read by her. Suddenly she cried—

"The novel-writers were all
serious people like you. They
are so hard on people like me.
They always make us come to
a bad end. They *say* we are
always acting, acting, acting;
and what else do you serious
people do? You act before the
world. I think, do you know, *we*
act before ourselves. All the old

foolish kings and queens in history were like us. They laughed
and beckoned and went to the
block for no very good purpose.
I dare say the headsmen were
like you."

"We would never cut off so
pretty a head."

" Oh, yes, you would — you
would cut off mine to-morrow."
All this she said vehemently,
piercing him with her bright eyes.
"You would cut off my head
to-morrow," she repeated, almost
fiercely; "I tell you you would."

Her departure was always unexpected, her moods changed with
so much rapidity. " Look!" she
said, pointing where the clock on
St. Peter's church showed above
the bushes. " Five minutes to
five. In five minutes my
mother's tea-hour. It is like
growing old. I go to gossip.
Good-bye."

The red feather shone for a
moment among the bushes and
was gone.

IV.

THE next day and the day after, Sherman was followed by those bright eyes. When he opened a letter at his desk they seemed to gaze at him from the open paper, and to watch him from the flies upon the ceiling. He was even a worse clerk than usual.

One evening he said to his mother, " Miss Leland has beautiful eyes."

" My dear, she puts belladonna in them."

" What a thing to say ! "

" I know she does, though her mother denies it."

" Well, she is certainly beautiful," he answered.

"My dear, if she has an attraction for you, I don't want to discourage it. She is rich as girls go nowadays; and one woman has one fault, another another: one's untidy, one fights with her servants, one fights with her friends, another has a crabbed tongue when she talks of them."

Sherman became again silent, finding no fragment of romance in such discourse.

In the next week or two he saw much of Miss Leland. He met her almost every evening on his return from the office, walking slowly, her racket under her arm. They played tennis much and talked more. Sherman began to play tennis in his dreams. Miss Leland told him all about herself, her friends, her inmost feelings; and yet every day he knew less about her. It was not merely that saying everything she said nothing, but that continually there came through her wild words the sound of the mys-

terious flutes and viols of that
unconscious nature which dwells
so much nearer to woman than
to man. How often do we not
endow the beautiful and candid
with depth and mystery not their
own? We do not know that we
but hear in their voices those
flutes and viols playing to us of
the alluring secret of the world.

Sherman had never known in
early life what is called first love,
and now, when he had passed
thirty, it came to him that love
more of the imagination than of
either the senses or affections: it
was mainly the eyes that followed him.

It is not to be denied that as
this love grew serious it grew
mercenary. Now active, now
latent, the notion had long been
in Sherman's mind, as we know,
that he should marry money. A
born lounger, riches tempted him
greatly. When those eyes haunted him from the fourteen flies on
the ceiling, he would say, " I
should be rich ; I should have a

house in the country; I should
hunt and shoot, and have a
garden and three gardeners; I
should leave this abominable
office." Then the eyes became
even more beautiful. It was a
new kind of belladonna.

He shrank a little, however,
from choosing even this pleasant
pathway. He had planned many
futures for himself and learnt to
love them all. It was this that
had made him linger on at Ballah
for so long, and it was this that
now kept him undecided. He
would have to give up the universe
for a garden and three gardeners.
How sad it was to make sub-
stantial even the best of his
dreams. How hard it was to
submit to that decree which com-
pels every step we take in life to
be a death in the imagination.
How difficult it was to be so
enwrapped in this one new hope
as not to hear the lamentations
that were going on in dim corners
of his mind.

One day he resolved to propose.

He examined himself in the glass
in the morning; and for the first
time in his life smiled to see
how good-looking he was.   In
the evening before leaving the
office he peered at himself in
the mirror over the mantlepiece
in the room where customers
were received.   The sun was
blazing through the window full
on his face.   He did not look so
well.   Immediately all courage
left him.

That evening he went out after
his mother had gone to bed and
walked far along the towing-path
of the Thames. A faint mist half
covered away the houses and fac-
tory chimneys on the further side;
beside him a band of osiers swayed
softly, the deserted and full river
lapping their stems. He looked on
all these things with foreign eyes.
He had no sense of possession.
Indeed it seemed to him that
everything in London was owned
by too many to be owned by
any one.   Another river that he
did seem to possess flowed

through his memory with all its
familiar sights—boys riding in
the stream to the saddle-girths,
fish leaping, water-flies raising
their small ripples, a swan asleep,
the wallflowers growing on the
red brick of the margin. He
grew very sad. Suddenly a
shooting star, fiery and vagabond,
leaped from the darkness. It
brought his mind again in a
moment to Margaret Leland.
To marry her, he thought, was
to separate himself from the old
life he loved so well.

Crossing the river at Putney,
he hurried homewards among
the market gardens. Nearing
home, the streets were deserted,
the shops closed. Where King
Street joins the Broadway, en-
tirely alone with itself, in the
very centre of the road a little
black cat was leaping after its
shadow.

"Ah!" he thought, "it would
be a good thing to be a little
black cat. To leap about in the
moonlight and sleep in the sun-

light, and catch flies, to have no hard tasks to do or hard decisions to come to; to be simple and full of animal spirits."

At the corner of Bridge Road was a coffee-stall, the only sign of human life. He bought some cold meat and flung it to the little black cat.

V.

SOME more days went by. At last, one day, arriving at the Square somewhat earlier than usual, and sitting down to wait for Margaret on the seat among the bushes, he noticed the pieces of a torn-up letter lying about. Beside him on the seat was a pencil, as though some one had been writing there and left it behind them. The pencil-lead was worn very short. The letter had been torn up, perhaps, in a fit of impatience.

In a half-mechanical way he glanced over the scraps. On one of them he read: "MY DEAR ELIZA,—What an incurable gossip

my mother is. You heard of my
misfortune. I nearly died——"
Here he had to search among
the scraps; at last he found one
that seemed to follow. " Perhaps you will hear news from
me soon. There is a handsome
young man who pays me atten-
tion, and——" Here another
piece had to be found. " I would
take him though he had a face
like the man in the moon, and
limped like the devil at the
theatre. Perhaps I am a little
in love. Oh! friend of my
heart——" Here it broke off
again. He was interested, and
searched the grass and the bushes
for fragments. Some had been
blown to quite a distance. He
got together several sentences
now. " I will not spend another
winter with my mother for anything. All this is, of course, a
secret. I had to tell somebody;
secrets are bad for my health.
Perhaps it will all come to
nothing." Then the letter went
off into dress, the last novel the

writer had read, and so forth. A Miss Sims, too, was mentioned, who had said some unkind thing of the writer.

Sherman was greatly amused. It did not seem to him wrong to read — we do not mind spying on one of the crowd, any more than on the personages of literature. It never occurred to him that he, or any friend of his, was concerned in these pencil scribblings.

Suddenly he saw this sentence: " Heigho ! your poor Margaret is falling in love again; condole with her, my dear."

He started. The name "Margaret," the mention of Miss Sims, the style of the whole letter, all made plain the authorship. Very desperately ashamed of himself, he got up and tore each scrap of paper into still smaller fragments and scattered them far apart.

That evening he proposed, and was accepted.

VI.

OR several days there was a new heaven and a new earth. Miss Leland seemed suddenly impressed with the seriousness of life. She was gentleness itself; and as Sherman sat on Sunday mornings in his pocket-handkerchief of a garden under the one tree, with its smoky stem, watching the little circles of sunlight falling from the leaves like a shower of new sovereigns, he gazed at them with a longer and keener joy than heretofore — a new heaven and a new earth, surely!

Sherman planted and dug and raked this pocket-handkerchief of a garden most diligently, root·

.ng out the docks and dande-
.ions and mouse-ear and the
patches of untimely grass. It
was the point of contact between
his new life and the old. It was
far too small and unfertile and
shaded in to satisfy his love of
gardener's experiments and early
vegetables.

Perforce this husbandry was
too little complex for his affections to gather much round plant
and bed. His garden in Ballah
used to touch him like the growth
of a young family.

Now he was content to satisfy
his barbaric sense of colour;
right round were planted alternate
holyhock and sunflower, and behind them scarlet-runners showed
their inch-high cloven shoots.

One Sunday it occurred to
him to write to his friends on
the matter of his engagement.
He numbered them over. Howard, one or two less intimate,
and Mary Carton. At that name
he paused; he would not write
just yet.

VII.

ONE Saturday there was a tennis party. Miss Leland devoted herself all day to a young Foreign Office clerk. She played tennis with him, talked with him, drank lemonade with him, had neither thoughts nor words for any one else. John Sherman was quite happy. Tennis was always a bore, and now he was not called upon to play. It had not struck him there was occasion for jealousy.

As the guests were dispersing, his betrothed came to him. Her manner seemed strange.

"Does anything ail you, Margaret?" he asked, as they left the Square.

"Everything," she answered, looking about her with ostentatious secrecy. "You are a most annoying person. You have no feeling; you have no temperament; you are quite the most stupid creature I was ever engaged to."

"What is wrong with you?" he asked, in bewilderment.

"Don't you see," she replied, with a broken voice, "I flirted all day with that young clerk? You should have nearly killed me with jealousy. You do not love me a bit! There is no knowing what I might do!"

"Well, you know," he said, "it was not right of you. People might say, 'Look at John Sherman; how furious he must be!' To be sure I wouldn't be furious a bit; but then they'd go about saying I was. It would not matter, of course; but you know it is not right of you."

"It is no use pretending you have feeling. It is all that miserable little town you come

from, with its sleepy old shops
and its sleepy old society. I
would give up loving you this
minute," she added, with a
caressing look, " if you had not
that beautiful bronzed face. I
will improve you. To-morrow
evening you must come to the
opera." Suddenly she changed
the subject. " Do you see that
little fat man coming out of the
Square and staring at me ? I
was engaged to him once. Look
at the four old ladies behind
him, shaking their bonnets at
me. Each has some story about
me, and it will be all the same
in a hundred years."

After this he had hardly a
moment's peace. She kept him
continually going to theatres,
operas, parties. These last were
an especial trouble ; for it was
her wont to gather about her an
admiring circle to listen to her
extravagancies, and he was no
longer at the age when we enjoy
audacity for its own sake.

VIII.

RADUALLY those bright eyes of his imagination, watching him from letters and from among the fourteen flies on the ceiling, had ceased to be centres of peace. They seemed like two whirlpools, wherein the order and quiet of his life were absorbed hourly and daily.

He still thought sometimes of the country house of his dreams and of the garden and the three gardeners, but somehow they had lost half their charm.

He had written to Howard and some others, and commenced, at last, a letter to Mary Carton. It lay unfinished on his desk ; a thin coating of dust was gathering upon it.

Mrs. Leland called continually on Mrs. Sherman. She sentimentalized over the lovers, and even wept over them; each visit supplied the household with conversation for a week.

Every Sunday morning—his letter-writing time — Sherman looked at his uncompleted letter. Gradually it became plain to him he could not finish it. It had never seemed to him he had more than friendship for Mary Carton, yet somehow it was not possible to tell her of this love-affair.

The more his betrothed troubled him the more he thought about the unfinished letter. He was a man standing at the cross-roads.

Whenever the wind blew from the south he remembered his friend, for that is the wind that fills the heart with memory.

One Sunday he removed the dust from the face of the letter almost reverently, as though it were the dust from the wheels of destiny. But the letter remained unfinished.

IX.

ONE Wednesday in June Sherman arrived home an hour earlier than usual from his office, as his wont was the first Wednesday in every month, on which day his mother was at home to her friends. They had not many callers. To-day there was no one as yet but a badly-dressed old lady his mother had picked up he knew not where. She had been looking at his photograph album, and recalling names and dates from her own prosperous times. As she went out Miss Leland came in. She gave the old lady in passing a critical look that made the poor creature very conscious of a threadbare mantle, and went over to Mrs. Sherman, holding out both hands. Sherman, who knew all his mother's peculiarities, noticed on her side a slight coldness; perhaps she did not altogether like this beautiful dragon-fly.

"I have come," said Miss Leland, "to tell John that he must learn to paint. Music and society are not enough. There is nothing like art to give refinement." Then turning to John Sherman—"My dear, I will make you quite different. You are a dreadful barbarian, you know."

"What ails me, Margaret?"

"Just look at that necktie! Nothing shows a man's cultivation like his necktie. Then your reading! You never read anything but old books nobody wants to talk about. I will lend you three every one has read this month. You really must acquire small talk and change your necktie."

Presently she noticed the

photograph-book lying open on a chair.

"Oh!" she cried, "I must have another look at John's beauties."

It was a habit of his to gather all manner of pretty faces. It came from incipient old bachelorhood, perhaps.

Margaret criticized each photo in turn with, "Ah! she looks as if she had some life in her!" or, "I do not like your sleepy eyelids," or some such phrase. The mere relations were passed by without a word. One face occurred several times—a quiet face. As Margaret came on this one for the third time, Mrs. Sherman, who seemed a little resentful about something, said—

"That is his friend, Mary Carton."

"He told me about her. He has a book she gave him. So that is she? How interesting! I pity these poor country people. It must be hard to keep from getting stupid."

"My friend is not at all stupid," said Sherman.

"Does she speak with a brogue? I remember you told me she was very good. It must be difficult to keep from talking platitudes when one is very good."

"You are quite wrong about her. You would like her very much," he replied.

"She is one of those people, I suppose, who can only talk about their relatives, or their families, or about their friends' children: how this one has got the hooping-cough, and this one is getting well of the measles!" She kept swaying one of the leaves between her finger and thumb impatiently. "What a strange way she does her hair; and what an ugly dress!"

"You must not talk that way about her—she is my great friend."

"Friend! friend!" she burst out. "He thinks I will believe in friendship between a man and a woman."

She got up, and said, turning round with an air of changing the subject, " Have you written to your friends about our engagement ? You had not done so when I asked you lately."

" I have."

" All ? "

" Well, not all."

" Your great friend, Miss—— what do you call her ? "

"Miss Carton. I have not written to her."

She tapped impatiently with her foot.

" They were really old companions—that is all," said Mrs. Sherman, wishing to mend matters. " They were both readers ; that brought them together. I never much fancied her. Yet she was well enough as a friend, and helped, maybe, with reading, and the gardening, and his good bringing-up, to keep him from the idle young men of the neighbourhood."

" You must make him write and tell her at once—you must,

you must!" almost sobbed out
Miss Leland.

"I promise," he answered.

Immediately returning to herself, she cried, "If I were in
her place I know what I would
like to do when I got the letter.
I know who I would like to kill!"
—this with a laugh as she went
over, and looked at herself in the
mirror over the mantlepiece.

PART III.

JOHN SHERMAN REVISITS BALLAH.

I.

HE others had gone, and Sherman was alone in the drawing-room by himself, looking through the window. Never had London seemed to him so like a reef whereon he was cast away. In the Square the bushes were covered with dust ; some sparrows were ruffling their feathers on the side-walk; people passed, con- tinually disturbing them. The sky was full of smoke. A terrible feeling of solitude in the midst of a multitude oppressed him. A portion of his life was ending. He thought that soon he would be no longer a young man, and now, at the period when the

desire of novelty grows less,
was coming the great change of
his life. He felt he was of
those whose granaries are in the
past. And now this past would
never renew itself. He was
going out into the distance as
though with strange sailors in a
strange ship.

He longed to see again the
town where he had spent his
childhood : to see the narrow
roads and mean little shops. And
perhaps it would be easier to tell
her who had been the friend of
so many years of this engagement in his own person than by
letter. He wondered why it
was so hard to write so simple
a thing.

It was his custom to act suddenly on his decisions. He had
not made many in his life.
The next day he announced at
the office that he would be absent
for three or four days. He told
his mother he had business in
the country.

His betrothed met him on the

way to the terminus, as he was
walking, bag in hand, and asked
where he was going. "I am
going on business to the country,"
he said, and blushed. He was.
creeping away like a thief.

II.

HE arrived in the town of Ballah by rail, for he had avoided the slow cattle steamer and gone by Dublin.

It was the forenoon, and he made for the Imperial Hotel to wait till four in the evening, when he would find Mary Carton in the school-house, for he had timed his journey so as to arrive on Thursday, the day of the children's practice.

As he went through the streets his heart went out to every familiar place and sight : the rows of tumble-down thatched cottages; the slated roofs of the shops; the women selling goose-

berries ; the river bridge ; the
high walls of the garden where
it was said the gardener used to
see the ghost of a former owner
in the shape of a rabbit ; the
street corner no child would
pass at nightfall for fear of the
headless soldier; the deserted
flour store; the wharves covered
with grass. All these he watched
with Celtic devotion, that devotion carried to the ends of the
world by the Celtic exiles, and
since old time surrounding their
journeyings with rumour of
plaintive songs.

He sat in the window of the
Imperial Hotel, now full of
guests. He did not notice any of
them. He sat there meditating,
meditating. Grey clouds covering the town with flying shadows
rushed by like the old and dis-
hevelled eagles that Maeldune saw
hurrying towards the waters of
life. Below in the street passed
by country people, townspeople,
travellers, women with baskets,
boys driving donkeys, old men

with sticks; sometimes he recognized a face or was recognized
himself, and welcomed by some
familiar voice.

" You have come home a handsomer gentleman than your father,
Misther John, and he was a
neat figure of a man, God bless
him ! " said the waiter, bringing
him his lunch ; and in truth
Sherman had grown handsomer
for these years away. His face
and gesture had more of dignity,
for on the centre of his nature
life had dropped a pinch of experience.

At four he left the hotel and
waited near the schoolhouse till
the children came running out.
One or two of the elder ones he
recognized but turned away.

III.

ARY CARTON was locking the harmonium as he went in. She came to meet him with a surprised and joyful air.

"How often I have wished to see you. When did you come? How well you remembered my habits to know where to find me. My dear John, how glad I am to see you."

"You are the same as when I left, and this room is the same, too."

"Yes," she answered, "the same, only I have had some new prints hung up—prints of fruits and leaves and bird-nests. It was only done last week.

When people choose pictures
and poems for children they
choose out such domestic ones.
I would not have any of the
kind; children are such un-
domestic animals. But, John,
I am so glad to see you in this
old schoolhouse again. So little
has changed with us here. Some
have died and some have been
married, and we are all a little
older and the trees a little
taller."

" I have come to tell you I
am going to be married."

She became in a moment
perfectly white, and sat down as
though attacked with faintness.
Her hand on the edge of the
chair trembled.

Sherman looked at her, and
went on· in a bewildered, mechanical way—"My betrothed is
a Miss Leland. She has a good
deal of money. You know my
mother always wished me to
marry some one with money.
Her father, when alive, was an
old client of Sherman and

Saunders. She is much admired
in society." Gradually his voice
became a mere murmur. He
did not seem to know that he
was speaking. He stopped en-
tirely. He was looking at Mary
Carton.

Everything around him was
as it had been some three
years before. The table was
covered with cups and the floor
with crumbs. Perhaps the
mouse pulling at a crumb under
the table was the same mouse
as on that other evening. The
only difference was the brooding
daylight of summer and the
ceaseless chirruping of the
sparrows in the ivy outside.
He had a confused sense of
having lost his way. It was
just the same feeling he had
known as a child, when one dark
night he had taken a wrong
turning, and instead of arriving
at his own house, found himself
at a landmark he knew was
miles from home.

A moment earlier, however

difficult his life, the issues were
always definite ; now suddenly
had entered the obscurity of
another's interest.

Before this it had not occurred
to him that Mary Carton had
any stronger feeling for him than
warm friendship.

He began again, speaking in
the same mechanical way—
" Miss Leland lives with her
mother near us. She is very
well educated and very well con-
nected, though she has lived
always among business people."

Miss Carton, with a great
effort, had recovered her com-
posure.

" I congratulate you," she
said. "I hope you will be
always happy. You came here
on some business for your firm, I
suppose ? I believe they have
some connection with the town
still."

" I only came here to tell you
I was going to be married."

" Do you not think it would
have been better to have

written?" she said, beginning to
put away the children's tea-
things in a cupboard by the fireplace.

"It would have been better,'
he answered, drooping his head.

Without a word, locking the
door behind them, they went
out.   Without a word they
walked the grey streets.   Now
and then a woman or a child
curtseyed as they passed.   Some
wondered, perhaps, to see these
old friends so silent.   At the
rectory they bade each other
good-bye.

"I hope you will be always
happy," she said.   "I will pray
for you and your wife.   I am
very busy with the children
and old people, but I shall
always find a moment to wish
you well in. Good-bye now."

They parted ; the gate in the
wall closed behind her.   He
stayed for a few moments looking up at the tops of the trees
and bushes showing over the
wall, and at the house a little

way beyond. He stood considering his problem—her life, his life. His, at any rate, would have incident and change; hers would be the narrow existence of a woman who, failing to fulfil the only abiding wish she has ever formed, seeks to lose herself in routine—mournfulest of things on this old planet.

This had been revealed: he loved Mary Carton, she loved him. He remembered Margaret Leland, and murmured she did well to be jealous. Then all her contemptuous words about the town and its inhabitants came into his mind. Once they made no impression on him, but now the sense of personal identity having been disturbed by this sudden revelation, alien as they were to his way of thinking, they began to press in on him. Mary, too, would have agreed with them, he thought; and might it be that at some distant time weary monotony in abandonment would have so weighed

down the spirit of Mary Carton,
that she would be merely one of
the old and sleepy whose dulness
filled the place like a cloud ?

He went sadly towards the
hotel ; everything about him, the
road, the sky, the feet wherewith
he walked seeming phantasmal
and without meaning.

He told the waiter he would
leave by the first train in the
morning. "What ! and you
only just come home?" the man
answered. He ordered coffee
and could not drink it. He
went out and came in again
immediately. He went down
into the kitchen and talked
to the servants. They told
him of everything that had
happened since he had gone.
He was not interested, and
went up to his room. " I must
go home and do what people
expect of me ; one must be care-
ful to do that."

Through all the journey
home his problem troubled him.
He saw the figure of Mary

6

Carton perpetually passing
through a round of monotonous
duties. He saw his own life among
aliens going on endlessly, wearily.

From Holyhead to London his
fellow-travellers were a lady and
her three young daughters, the
eldest about twelve. The smooth
faces shining with well-being
became to him ominous symbols.
He hated them. They were
symbolic of the indifferent world
about to absorb him, and of
the vague something that was
dragging him inch by inch from
the nook he had made for himself in the chimney corner. He
was at one of those dangerous
moments when the sense of
personal identity is shaken, when
one's past and present seem
about to dissolve partnership.
He sought refuge in memory,
and counted over every word of
Mary's he could remember. He
forgot the present and the future.
" Without love," he said to himself, " we would be either gods
or vegetables."

The rain beat on the window of the carriage. He began to listen ; thought and memory became a blank; his mind was full of the sound of rain-drops.

PART IV.

THE REV. WILLIAM HOWARD.

I.

AFTER his return to London Sherman for a time kept to himself, going straight home from his office, moody and self-absorbed, trying not to consider his problem—her life, his life. He often repeated to himself, " I must do what people expect of me. It does not rest with me now—my choosing time is over." He felt that whatever way he turned he would do a great evil to himself and others. To his nature all sudden decisions were difficult, and so he kept to the groove he had entered upon. It did not even occur to him to do otherwise. He never thought of

breaking this engagement off
and letting people say what they
would. He was bound in hopelessly by a chain of congratula-
tions.

A week passed slowly as a
month. The wheels of the cabs
and carriages seemed to be rolling through his mind. He often
remembered the quiet river at
the end of his garden in the
town of Ballah. How the weeds
swayed there, and the salmon
leaped ! At the week's end
came a note from Miss Leland,
complaining of his neglecting
her so many days. He sent a
rather formal answer, promising
to call soon. To add to his
other troubles a cold east wind
arose and made him shiver continually.

One evening he and his mother
were sitting silent, the one knitting, the other half-asleep. He
had been writing letters and was
now in a reverie. Round the
walls were one or two drawings,
done by him at school. His

mother had got them framed. His eyes were fixed on a drawing of a stream and some astonishing cows.

A few days ago he had found an old sketch-book for children among some forgotten papers, which taught how to draw a horse by making three ovals for the basis of his body, one lying down in the middle, two standing up at each end for flank and chest, and how to draw a cow by basing its body on a square. He kept trying to fit squares into the cows. He was half inclined to take them out of their frames and retouch on this new principle. Then he began somehow to remember the child with the swollen face who threw a stone at the dog the day he resolved to leave home first. Then some other image came. His problem moved before him in a disjointed way. He was dropping asleep. Through his reverie came the click, click of his mother's needles. She had

found some London children to
knit for.   He   was   at   that
marchland between waking and
dreaming where our thoughts begin to have a life of their own—
the region where art is nurtured
and inspiration born.

He started, hearing something
sliding and rustling, and looked
up to see a piece of cardboard
fall from one end of the mantlepiece, and, driven by a slight gust
of air, circle into the ashes under
the grate.

" Oh," said his mother, " that
is   the   portrait   of   the   *locum
tenens.*"   She still spoke of the
Rev. William Howard by the
name she had first known him
by.   " He is always being photo-
graphed.   They are all over the
house, and I, an old woman, have
not had one taken all my life.
Take it out with the tongs."
Her son after some poking in
the ashes, for it had fallen far
back, brought out a somewhat
dusty photograph.   " That," she
continued, " is one he sent us

two or three months ago. It
has been lying in the letter-rack
since."

"He is not so spick and span
looking as usual," said Sherman,
rubbing the ashes off the photograph with his sleeve.

"By the by," his mother replied, "he has lost his parish, I
hear. He is very mediæval, you
know, and he lately preached a
sermon to prove that children
who die unbaptized are lost. He
had been reading up the subject
and was full of it. The mothers
turned against him, not being so
familiar with St. Augustine as he
was. There were other reasons
in plenty too. I wonder that
any one can stand that mon-
keyish fantastic family."

As the way is with so many
country-bred people, the world
for her was divided up into
families rather than individuals.

While she was talking, Sherman, who had returned to his
chair, leant over the table and
began to write hurriedly. She

was continuing her denuncia-
tion when he interrupted with—
"Mother, I have just written this
letter to him :—

"'MY DEAR HOWARD:
"'Will you come and spend the
autumn with us? I hear you
are unoccupied just now. I am
engaged to be married, as you
know; it will be a long engagement. You will like my betrothed. I hope you will be
great friends.
"'Yours expectantly,
"'JOHN SHERMAN.'"

"You rather take me aback,"
she said.
"I really like him," he answered. "You were always pre-
judiced against the Howards.
Forgive me, but I really want
very much to have him here."
"Well, if you like him, I suppose I have no objection."
"I do like him. He is very
clever," said her son, "and
knows a great deal. I wonder

he does not marry. Do you not think he would make a good husband ?—for you must admit he is sympathetic."

" It is not difficult to sympa-- thize with every one if you have no true principles and convic- tions."

Principles and convictions were her names for that strenuous con- sistency attained without trouble by men and women of few ideas.

" I am sure you will like him better," said the other, " when you see more of him."

" Is that photograph quite spoilt ? " she answered.

" No ; there was nothing on it but ashes."

" That is a pity, for one less would be something."

After this they both became silent, she knitting, he gazing at the cows browsing at the edge of their stream, and trying to fit squares into their bodies ; but now a smile played about his lips.

Mrs. Sherman looked a little

troubled. She would not object to any visitor of her son's, but quite made up her mind in no manner to put herself out to entertain the Rev. William Howard. She was puzzled as well. She did not understand the suddenness of this invitation. They usually talked over things for weeks.

II.

EXT day his fellow-clerks noticed a decided improvement in Sherman's spirits. He had a lark-like cheerfulness and alacrity breaking out at odd moments. When evening came he called, for the first time since his return, on Miss Leland. She scolded him roundly for having answered her note in such a formal way, but was sincerely glad to see him return to his allegiance. We have said he had sometimes, though rarely, a talkative fit. He had one this evening. The last play they had been to, the last party, the picture of the year, all in turn he glanced at.

She was delighted. Her training had not been in vain. Her barbarian was learning to chatter. This flattered her a deal.

"I was never engaged," she thought, "to a more interesting creature."

When he had risen to go Sherman said—"I have a friend coming to visit me in a few days; you will suit each other delightfully. He is very mediæval."

"Do tell me about him; I like everything mediæval."

"Oh," he cried, with a laugh, "his mediævalism is not in your line. He is neither a gay troubadour nor a wicked knight. He is a High Church curate."

"Do not tell me anything more about him," she answered; "I will try to be civil to him, but you know I never liked curates. I have been an agnostic for many years. You, I believe, are orthodox."

As Sherman was on his way home he met a fellow-clerk, and stopped him with—

"Are you an agnostic?"

"No.   Why, what is that?"

"Oh, nothing! Good-bye," he made answer, and hurried on his way.

III.

THE letter reached the Rev. William Howard at the right moment, arriving as it did in the midst of a crisis in his fortunes. In the course of a short life he had lost many parishes. He considered himself a martyr, but was considered by his enemies a clerical coxcomb. He had a habit of getting his mind possessed with some strange opinion, or what seemed so to his parishioners, and of preaching it while the notion lasted in the most startling way. The sermon on unbaptized children was an instance. It was not so much that he thought it true as that it possessed

him for a day. It was not so
much the thought as his own
relation to it that allured him.
Then, too, he loved what appeared to his parishioners to be
the most unusual and dangerous
practices. He put candles on the
altar and crosses in unexpected
places. He delighted in the
intricacies of High Church cos-
tume, and was known to recom-
mend confession and prayers
for the dead.

Gradually the anger of his
parishioners would increase.
The rector, the washerwoman,
the labourers, the squire, the
doctor, the school teachers, the
shoemakers, the butchers, the
seamstresses, the local journalist,
the master of the hounds, the
innkeeper, the veterinary sur-
geon, the magistrate, the children making mud pies, all would
be filled with one dread—popery.
Then he would fly for consolation
to his little circle of the faithful,
the younger ladies, who still repeated his fine sentiments and

saw him in their imaginations
standing perpetually before a wall
covered with tapestry and holding a crucifix in some constrained
and ancient attitude. At last he
would have to go, feeling for his
parishioners a gay and lofty dis-
dain, and for himself that reve-
rend approbation one gives to the
captains who lead the crusade of
ideas against those who merely
sleep and eat. An efficient cru-
sader he certainly was — too
efficient, indeed, for his efficiency
gave to all his thoughts a certain over-completeness and isola-
tion, and a kind of hardness to his
mind. His intellect was like a
musician's instrument with no
sounding-board. He could think
carefully and cleverly, and even
with originality, but never in such
a way as to make his thoughts an
allusion to something deeper than
themselves. In this he was the
reverse of poetical, for poetry is
essentially a touch from behind a
curtain.

This conformation of his mind

helped to lead him into all manner
of needless contests and to the
loss of this last parish among
much else.   Did not the world
exist for the sake of these hard,
crystalline thoughts, with which
he played as with so many bone
spilikins, delighting in his own
skill? and were not all who dis-
liked them merely—the many?

In this way it came about that
Sherman's letter reached Howard
at the right moment.   Now, next
to a new parish, he loved a new
friend.   A visit to London meant
many.   He had found he was, on
the whole, a success at the beginning of friendships.

He at once wrote an acceptance
in his small and beautiful hand-
writing, and arrived shortly after
his letter.   Sherman, on receiving
him, glanced at his neat and
shining boots, the little medal at
the watch-chain and the well-
brushed hat, and nodded as though
in answer to an inner query.   He
smiled approval at the slight,
elegant figure in its black clothes,

at the satiny hair, and at the face, mobile as moving waters.

For several days the Shermans saw little of their guest. He had friends everywhere to turn into enemies and acquaintances to turn into friends. His days passed in visiting, visiting, visiting. Then there were theatres and churches to see, and new clothes to be bought, over which he was as anxious as a woman. Finally he settled down.

He passed his mornings in the smoking-room. He asked Sherman's leave to hang on the walls one or two religious pictures, without which he was not happy, and to place over the mantle-piece, under the pipe-rack, an ebony crucifix. In one corner of the room he laid a rug neatly folded for covering his knees on chilly days, and on the table a small collection of favourite books—a curious and carefully-chosen collection, in which Cardinal Newman and Bourget, St. Chrysostom and Flaubert,

lived together in perfect friendship.

Early in his visit Sherman
brought him to the Lelands. He
was a success. The three—Margaret, Sherman, and Howard—
played tennis in the Square.
Howard was a good player, and
seemed to admire Margaret. On
the way home Sherman once or
twice laughed to himself. It was
like the clucking of a hen with
a brood of chickens. He told
Howard, too, how wealthy Margaret was said to be.

After this Howard always joined
Sherman and Margaret at the
tennis. Sometimes, too, after a
little, on days when the study
seemed dull and lonely, and the
unfinished essay on St. Chrysostom more than usually laborious,
he would saunter towards the
Square before his friend's arrival,
to find Margaret now alone, now
with an acquaintance or two.
About this time also press of
work, an unusual thing with him,
began to delay Sherman in town

half an hour after his usual time.
In the evenings they often talked
of Margaret — Sherman frankly
and carefully, as though in all
anxiety to describe her as she
was; and Howard with some
enthusiasm: "She has a religious
vocation," he said once, with a
slight sigh.

Sometimes they played chess—
a game that Sherman had re-
cently become devoted to, for he
found it drew him out of himself
more than anything else.

Howard now began to notice a
curious thing. Sherman grew
shabbier and shabbier, and at
the same time more and more
cheerful. This puzzled him, for
he had noticed that he himself
was not cheerful when shabby,
and did not even feel upright and
clever when his hat was getting
old. He also noticed that when
Sherman was talking to him
he seemed to be keeping some
thought to himself. When he
first came to know him long ago
in Ballah he had noticed occa-

sionally the same thing, and set
it down to a kind of suspicious-
ness and over-caution, natural to
one who lived in such an out-of-
the-way place. It seemed more
persistent now, however. " He
is not well trained," he thought;.
" he is half a peasant. He has
not the brilliant candour of the
man of the world."

All this while the mind of
Sherman was clucking continually
over its brood of thoughts. Ballah
was being constantly suggested
to him. The grey corner of a
cloud slanting its rain upon
Cheapside called to mind by
some remote suggestion the
clouds rushing and falling in
cloven surf on the seaward steep
of a mountain north of Ballah.
A certain street corner made him
remember an angle of the Ballah
fish-market. At night a lantern,.
marking where the road was
fenced off for mending, made him
think of a tinker's cart, with its
swing can of burning coals, that
used to stop on market days at

the corner of Peter's Lane at
Ballah. Delayed by a crush in the
Strand, he heard a faint trickling
of water near by; it came from
a shop window where a little
water-jet balanced a wooden ball
upon its point. The sound suggested a cataract with a long
Gaelic name, that leaped crying
into the Gate of the Winds at
Ballah. Wandering among these
memories a footstep went to
and fro continually and the figure
of Mary Carton moved among
them like a phantom. He was
set dreaming a whole day
by walking down one Sunday
morning to the border of the
Thames—a few hundred yards
from his house—and looking at
the osier-covered Chiswick eyot.
It made him remember an old
day-dream of his. The source
of the river that passed his garden
at home was a certain wood-
bordered and islanded lake,
whither in childhood he had
often gone blackberry-gathering.
At the further end was a little islet

called Inniscrewin. Its rocky
centre, covered with many bushes,
rose some forty feet above the
lake. Often when life and its
difficulties had seemed to him
like the lessons of some elder
boy given to a younger by mis-
take, it had seemed good to
dream of going away to that
islet and building a wooden hut
there and burning a few years
out, rowing to and fro, fishing,
or lying on the island slopes by
day, and listening at night to
the ripple of the water and the
quivering of the bushes — full
always of unknown creatures—
and going out at morning to see
the island's edge marked by the
feet of birds.

These pictures became so vivid
to him that the world about
him—that Howard, Margaret,
his mother even—began to seem
far off. He hardly seemed aware
of anything they were thinking
and feeling. The light that
dazzled him flowed from the
vague and refracting regions of

hope and memory; the light that made Howard's feet unsteady was ever the too glaring lustre of life itself.

IV.

N the evening of the 20th of June, after the blinds had been pulled down and the gas lighted, Sherman was playing chess in the smoking-room, right hand against left. Howard had gone out with a message to the Lelands. He would often say, " Is there any message I can deliver for you? I know how lazy you are, and will save you the trouble." A message was always found for him. A pile of books lent for Sherman's improvement went home one by one.

"Look here," said Howard's voice in the doorway, "I have been watching you for some time.

You are cheating the red men
most villainously. You are
forcing them to make mistakes
that the white men may win.
Why, a few such games would
ruin any man's moral nature."

He was leaning against the
doorway, looking, to Sherman's
not too critical eyes, an embodi-
ment of all that was self-possessed
and brilliant. The great care
with which he was dressed and
his whole manner seemed to say,
"Look at me; do I not combine
perfectly the zealot with the man
of the world?" He seemed excited to-night. He had been
talking at the Lelands, and
talking well, and felt that elation
which brings us many thoughts.

"My dear Sherman," he went
on, "do cease that game. It is
very bad for you. There is nobody alive who is honest enough
to play a game of chess fairly
out—right hand against left.
We are so radically dishonest
that we even cheat ourselves.
We can no more play chess

than we can think altogether by ourselves with security. You had much better play with me."

"Very well, but you will beat me; I have not much practice," replied the other.

They reset the men and began to play. Sherman relied most upon his bishops and queen. Howard was fondest of the knights. At first Sherman was the attacking party, but in his characteristic desire to scheme out his game many moves ahead, kept making slips, and at last had to give up, with his men nearly all gone and his king hopelessly cornered. Howard seemed to let nothing escape him. When the game was finished he leant back in his chair and said, as he rolled a cigarette—

"You do not play well." It gave him satisfaction to feel his proficiency in many small arts. "You do not do any of these things at all well," he went on, with an insolence peculiar to him when excited. "You have been really very badly brought up and stupidly educated in that intolerable Ballah. They do not understand there any, even the least, of the arts of life; they only believe in information. Men who are compelled to move in the great world, and who are also cultivated, only value the personal acquirements—self-possession, adaptability, how to dress well, how even to play tennis decently—you would be not so bad at that, by the by, if you practised—or how to paint or write effectively. They know that it is better to smoke one's cigarette with a certain charm of gesture than to have by heart all the encyclopedias. I say this not merely as a man of the world, but as a teacher of religion. A man when he rises from the grave will take with him only the things that he is in himself. He will leave behind the things that he merely possesses, learning and information not less than money and high estate. They will stay behind with his house and his clothes and his body. A collection of facts will no more help him than a collection of stamps. The learned will not get into heaven as readily as the flute-player, or even as the man who smokes a cigarette gracefully. Now you are not learned, but you have been brought up almost as badly as if you were. In that wretched town they told you that education was to know that Russia is bounded on the north by the Arctic Sea, and on the west by the Baltic Ocean, and that Vienna is situated on the Danube, and that William the Third came to the throne in the year 1688. They have never taught you any personal art. Even chess-playing might have helped you at the day of judgment."

"I am really not a worse chess-player than you. I am only more careless."

There was a slight resentment
in Sherman's voice. The other
noticed it, and said, changing
his manner from the insolent
air of a young beauty to a self-
depreciatory one, which was wont
to give him at times a very
genuine charm—

"It is really a great pity, for
you Shermans are a deep people,
much deeper than we Howards.
We are like moths or butterflies
on rather rapid rivulets, while
you and yours are deep pools in
the forest where the beasts go to
drink.   No! I have a better
metaphor.   Your mind and mine
are two arrows. Yours has got
no feathers, and mine has no
metal on the point. I don't know
which is most needed for right
conduct.   I wonder where we
are going to strike earth.   I
suppose it will be all right some
day when the world has gone by
and they have collected all the
arrows into one quiver."

He went over to the mantlepiece to hunt for a match, as

his cigarette had gone out.
Sherman had lifted a corner of
the blind and was gazing over
the roofs shining from a recent
shower, and thinking how on
such a night as this he had sat
with Mary Carton by the rectory
fire listening to the rain without
and talking of the future and of
the training of village children.

"Have you seen Miss Leland
in her last new dress from
Paris?" said Howard, making
one of his rapid transitions.
"It is very rich in colour, and
makes her look a little pale, like
St. Cecilia. She is wonderful as
she stands by the piano, a silver
cross round her neck. We have
been talking about you. She
complains to me. She says you
are a little barbarous; you seem
to look down on style, and sometimes—you must forgive me—
even on manners, and you are
quite without small talk. You
must really try and be worthy of
that beautiful girl, with her great
soul and religious genius. She

told me quite sadly, too, that you are not improving."

" No," said Sherman, " I am not going forward; I am at present trying to go sideways like the crabs."

" Be serious," answered the other. " She told me these things with the most sad and touching voice. She makes me her confidant, you know, in many matters, because of my wide religious experience. You must really improve yourself. You must paint or something."

" Well, I will paint or something."

" I am quite serious, Sherman. Try and be worthy of her, a soul as gentle as St. Cecilia's."

" She is very wealthy," said Sherman. " If she were engaged to you and not to me you might hope to die a bishop."

Howard looked at him in a mystified way and the conversation dropped. Presently Howard got up and went to his room, and Sherman, resetting the chess-board, began to play again, and, letting longer and longer pauses of reverie come between his moves, played far into the morning, cheating now in favour of the red men now in. favour of the white.

V.

THE next afternoon Howard found Miss Leland sitting, reading in an alcove in her drawing-room, between a stuffed paroquet and a blue De Morgan jar. As he was shown in he noticed, with a momentary shock, that her features were quite commonplace. Then she saw him, and at once seemed to vanish wrapped in an exulting flame of life. She stood up, flinging the book on to the seat with some violence.

"I have been reading that sweet 'Imitation of Christ,' and was just feeling that I should have to become a theosophist or a socialist, or go and join the

Catholic Church, or do something.
How delightful it is to see you
again! How is my savage getting on? It is so good of you to
try and help me to reform him."

They talked on about Sherman,
and Howard did his best to con-
sole her for his shortcomings.
Time would certainly improve
her savage. Several times she
gazed at him with those large
dark eyes of hers, of which the
pupils to-day seemed larger than
usual. They made him feel dizzy
and clutch tightly the arm of his
chair. Then she began to talk
about her life since childhood—
how they got to the subject he
never knew—and made a number
of those confidences which are so
dangerous because so flattering.
To love—there is nothing else
worth living for; but then men
are so shallow. She had never
found a nature deep as her own.
She would not pretend that she
had not often been in love, but
never had any heart rung back
to her the true note. As she

spoke her face quivered with excitement. The exulting flame of life seemed spreading from her to the other things in the room. To Howard's eyes it seemed as though the bright pots and stuffed birds and plush curtains began to glow with a light not of this world—to glimmer like the strange and chaotic colours the mystic Blake imagined upon the scaled serpent of Eden. The light seemed gradually to dim his past and future, and to make pale his good resolves. Was it not in itself that which all men are seeking, and for which all else exists ?

He leant forward and took her hand, timidly and doubtingly. She did not draw it away. He leant nearer and kissed her on the forehead. She gave a joyful cry, and, casting her arms round his neck, burst out, "Ah! you—and I. We were made for each other. I hate Sherman. He is an egotist. He is a beast. He is selfish and foolish." Releas-

ing one of her arms she struck
the seat with her hand, excitedly,
and went on, " How angry he will
be! But it serves him right! How
badly he is dressing. He does
not know anything about anything. But you—you—I knew
you were meant for me the moment I saw you."

That evening Howard flung
himself into a chair in the empty
smoking-room.   He lighted a
cigarette; it went out.   Again he
lighted it; again it went out. " I
am   a   traitor—and   that good,
stupid fellow, Sherman, never to
be jealous!" he thought.   " But
then, how could I help it ?   And,.
besides, it cannot be a bad action
to save her from a man she is so
much above in refinement and feeling."   He was getting into good-
humour with himself.   He got up
and went over and looked at the
photograph of Raphael's Ma-
donna, which he had hung over
the   mantlepiece.   " How like
Margaret's are her big eyes ! "

VI.

THE next day when Sherman came home from his office he saw an envelope lying on the smoking-room table. It contained a letter from Howard, saying that he had gone away, and that he hoped Sherman would forgive his treachery, but that he was hopelessly in love with Miss Leland, and that she returned his love.

Sherman went downstairs. His mother was helping the servant to set the table.

"You will never guess what has happened," he said. "My affair with Margaret is over."

"I cannot pretend to be sorry, John," she replied. She had

long considered Miss Leland
among accepted things, like the
chimney-pots on the roof, and
submitted, as we do, to any un-
alterable fact, but had never
praised her or expressed liking
in any way. "She puts belladonna in her eyes, and is a vixen
and a flirt, and I dare say her
wealth is all talk. But how did
it happen ? "

Her son was, however, too
excited to listen.

He went upstairs and wrote
the following note—

"MY DEAR MARGARET :
"I congratulate you on a new
conquest. There is no end to
your victories. As for me, I bow
myself out with many sincere
wishes for your happiness, and
remain,
"Your friend,
"JOHN SHERMAN."

Having posted this letter he
sat down with Howard's note
spread out before him, and won-

dered whether there was anything
mean and small-minded in neat-
ness—he himself was somewhat
untidy. He had often thought
so before, for their strong friendship was founded in a great
measure on mutual contempt,
but now immediately added,
being in good-humour with the
world, "He is much cleverer
than I am. He must have been
very industrious at school."

A week went by. He made
up his mind to put an end to his
London life. He broke to his
mother his resolve to return to
Ballah. She was delighted, and
at once began to pack. Her old
home had long seemed to her a
kind of lost Eden, wherewith
she was accustomed to contrast
the present. When, in time, this
present had grown into the past
it became an Eden in turn. She
was always ready for a change,
if the change came to her in the
form of a return to something old.
Others place their ideals in the
future ; she laid hers in the past.

The only one this momentous resolution seemed to surprise was the old and deaf servant. She waited with ever - growing impatience. She would sit by the hour wool-gathering on the corner of a chair with a look of bewildered delight. As the hour of departure came near she sang continually in a cracked voice.

Sherman, a few days before leaving, was returning for the last time from his office when he saw, to his surprise, Howard and Miss Leland carrying each a brown paper bundle. He nodded good - humouredly, meaning to pass on.

"John," she said, "look at this brooch William gave me—a ladder leaning against the moon and a butterfly climbing up it. Is it not sweet? We are going to visit the poor."

"And I," he said, "am going to catch eels. I am leaving town."

He made his excuses, saying he had no time to wait, and

hurried off. She looked after him with a mournful glance, strange in anybody who had exchanged one lover for another more favoured.

"Poor fellow," murmured Howard, "he is broken-hearted."

"Nonsense," answered Miss Leland, somewhat snappishly.

PART V.

JOHN SHERMAN RETURNS TO BALLAH.

THIS being the homeward trip, SS. *Lavinia* carried no cattle, but many passengers. As the sea was smooth and the voyage near its end, they lounged about the deck in groups. Two cattle merchants were leaning over the taffrail smoking. In appearance they were something between betting men and commercial travellers. For years they had done all their sleeping in steamers and trains. A short distance from them a clerk from Liverpool, with a consumptive cough, walked to and fro, a little child holding his hand. Shortly he would be landed in a boat putting off from

the shore for the purpose. He
had come hoping that his native
air of Teeling Head would
restore him. The little child
was a strange contrast — her
cheeks ruddy with perfect health.
Further forward, talking to one
of the crew, was a man with a
red face and slightly unsteady
step. In the companion house
was a governess, past her first
youth, very much afraid of sea-
sickness. She had brought her
luggage up and heaped it round
her to be ready for landing.
Sherman sat on a pile of cable
looking out over the sea. It was
just noon; SS. *Lavinia*, having
passed by Tory and Rathlin, was
approaching the Donegal cliffs.
They were covered by a faint
mist, which made them loom
even vaster than they were. To
westward the sun shone on a
perfectly blue sea. Seagulls
come out of the mist and
plunged into the sunlight, and
out of the sunlight and plunged
into the mist. To the westward

gannets were striking continually,
and a porpoise showed now and
then, his fin and back gleaming
in the sun. Sherman was more
perfectly happy than he had been
for many a day, and more ar-
dently thinking. All nature
seemed full of a Divine fulfilment. Everything fulfilled its
law—fulfilment that is peace,
whether it be for good or for evil,
for evil also has its peace, the
peace of the birds of prey.
Sherman looked from the sea
to the ship and grew sad. Upon
this thing, crawling slowly along
the sea, moved to and fro many
mournful and slouching figures.
He looked from the ship to himself and his eyes filled with
tears. On himself, on these
moving figures, hope and memory
fed like flames.

Again his eyes gladdened, for
he knew he had found his present.
He would live in his love and the
day as it passed. He would live
that his law might be fulfilled.
Now, was he sure of this truth ?

—the saints on the one hand, the
animals on the other, live in the
moment as it passes. Thither-
ward had his days brought him.
This was the one grain they had
ground. To grind one grain is
sufficient for a lifetime.

II.

 FEW days later Sherman was hurrying through the town of Ballah. It was Saturday, and he passed down through the marketing country people, and the old women with baskets of cakes and gooseberries and long pieces of sugarstick shaped like walking-sticks, and called by children "Peggie's leg."

Now, as two months earlier he was occasionally recognized and greeted, and, as before, went on without knowing, his eyes full of unintelligent sadness because the mind was making merry afar. They had the look we see in the eyes of animals and dreamers.

Everything had grown simple,
his problem had taken itself
away. He was thinking what he
would say to Mary Carton. Now
they would be married, they
would live in a small house with
a green door and new thatch,
and a row of beehives under a
hedge. He knew where just
such a house stood empty. The
day before he and his mother
had discussed, with their host of
the Imperial Hotel, this question
of houses. They knew the peculiarities of every house in the
neighbourhood, except two or
three built while they were away.
All day Sherman and his mother
had gone over the merits of the
few they were told were empty.
She wondered why her son had
grown so unpractical. Once he
was so easily pleased—the row
of beehives and the new thatch
did not for her settle the question.
She set it all down to Miss
Leland and the plays, and the
singing, and the belladonna, and
remembered with pleasure how

many miles of uneasy water lay
between the town of Ballah and
these things.

She did not know what else
beside the row of beehives and
the new thatch her son's mind
ran on as he walked among the
marketing country people, and
the gooseberry sellers, and the
merchants of "Peggie's leg,"
and the boys playing marbles in
odd corners, and the men in
waistcoats with flannel sleeves
driving carts, and the women
driving donkeys with creels of
turf or churns of milk. Just now
she was trying to remember
whether she used to buy her
wool for knitting at Miss Peters's
or from Mrs. Macallough's at the
bridge. One or other sold it a
halfpenny a skein cheaper. She
never knew what went on inside
her son's mind, she had always
her own fish to fry. Blessed are
the unsympathetic. They pre-
serve their characters in an iron
safe while the most of us poor
mortals are going about the

planet vainly searching for any
kind of a shell to contain us, and
evaporating the while.

Sherman began to mount the
hill to the vicarage. He was
happy. Because he was happy
he began to run. Soon the
steepness of the hill made him
walk. He thought about his love
for Mary Carton. Seen by the
light of this love everything
that had happened to him was
plain now. He had found his
centre of unity. His childhood
had prepared him for this love.
He had been solitary, fond of
favourite corners of fields, fond
of going about alone, unhuman
like the birds and the leaves, his
heart empty. How clearly he
remembered his first meeting
with Mary. They were both
children. At a school treat they
watched the fire balloon ascend,
and followed it a little way over
the fields together. What friends
they became, growing up together, reading the same books,
thinking the same thoughts.

As he came to the door and pulled at the great hanging iron bell handle, the fire balloon re-ascended in his heart, surrounded with cheers and laughter.

III.

E kept the servant talking for a moment or two before she went for Miss Carton. The old rector, she told him, was getting less and less able to do much work. Old age had come almost suddenly upon him. He seldom moved from the fireside. He was getting more and more absent-minded. Once lately he had brought his umbrella into the reading-desk. More and more did he leave all things to his children—to Mary Carton and her younger sisters.

When the servant had gone Sherman looked round the somewhat gloomy room. In the window hung a canary in a

painted cage. Outside was a
narrow piece of shaded ground
between the window and the
rectory wall. The laurel and
holly bushes darkened the win--
dow a good deal. On a table in
the centre of the room were
evangelistic books with gilded
covers. Round the mirror over
the mantlepiece were stuck
various parish announcements,
thrust between the glass and the
gilding. On a small side table
was a copper ear-trumpet.

How familiar everything
seemed to Sherman. Only the
room seemed smaller than it did
three years before, and close to
the table with the ear-trumpet,
at one side of the fireplace before
the arm-chair, was a new thread--
bare patch in the carpet.

Sherman recalled how in this
room he and Mary Carton had
sat in winter by the fire, building
castles in the air for each other.
So deeply meditating was he
that she came in and stood
unnoticed beside him.

"John," she said at last, "it is a great pleasure to see you so soon again. Are you doing well in London?"

"I have left London."

"Are you married, then? You must introduce me to your wife."

"I shall never be married to Miss Leland."

"What?"

"She has preferred another— my friend William Howard. I have come here to tell you something, Mary." He went and stood close to her and took her hand tenderly. "I have always been very fond of you. Often in London, when I was trying to think of another kind of life, I used to see this fireside and you sitting beside it, where we used to sit and talk about the future. Mary —Mary," he held her hand in both his—"you will be my wife?"

"You do not love me, John," she answered, drawing herself away. "You have come to me because you think it your duty.

I have had nothing but duty all
my life."

"Listen," he said. "I was very
miserable ; I invited Howard to
stay with us. One morning I
found a note on the smoking-
room table to say that Margaret
had accepted him, and I have
come here to ask you to marry
me. I never cared for any one
else."

He found himself speaking
hurriedly, as though anxious to
get the words said and done with.
It now seemed to him that he
had done ill in this matter of
Miss Leland. He had not before
thought of it — his mind had
always been busy with other
things. Mary Carton looked at
him wonderingly.

" John," she said at last, " did
you ask Mr. Howard to stay
with you on purpose to get him
to fall in love with Miss Leland,
or to give you an excuse for
breaking off your engagement, as
you knew he flirted with every
one ? "

"Margaret seems very fond of him. I think they are made for each other," he answered.

"Did you ask him to London on purpose?"

"Well, I will tell you," he faltered. "I was very miserable. I had drifted into this engagement I don't know how. Margaret glitters and glitters and glitters, but she is not of my kind. I suppose I thought, like a fool, I should marry some one who was rich. I found out soon that I loved nobody but you. I got to be always thinking of you and of this town. Then I heard that Howard had lost his curacy, and asked him up. I just left them alone and did not go near Margaret much. I knew they were made for each other. Do not let us talk of them," he continued, eagerly. "Let us talk about the future. I will take a farm and turn farmer. I dare say my uncle will not give me anything when he dies because I have left his office. He will call

me a ne'er-do-weel, and say I
would squander it. But you and
I—we will get married, will we
not ? We will be very happy,"
he went on, pleadingly. " You
will still have your charities, and
I shall be busy with my farm.
We will surround ourselves with
a wall. The world will be on the
outside, and on the inside we and
our peaceful lives."

"Wait," she said ; "I will give
you your answer," and going into
the next room returned with
several bundles of letters. She
laid them on the table ; some
were white and new, some
slightly yellow with time.

"John," she said, growing very
pale, " here are all the letters
you ever wrote me from your
earliest boyhood." She took one
of the large candles from the
mantlepiece, and, lighting it,
placed it on the hearth. Sherman wondered what she was
going to do with it. " I will
tell you," she went on, " what
I had thought to carry to the

grave unspoken. I have loved
you for a long time. When you
came and told me you were
going to be married to another
I forgave you, for man's love is
like the wind, and I prayed that
God might bless you both." She
leant down over the candle, her
face pale and contorted with
emotion. ".All these letters
after that grew very sacred.
Since we were never to be
married they grew a portion of
my life, separated from everything and every one—a something apart and holy. I re-read
them all, and arranged them in
little bundles according to their
dates, and tied them with thread.
Now I and you—we have nothing
to do with each other any more."

She held the bundle of letters
in the flame. He got up from his
seat. She motioned him away
imperiously. He looked at the
flame in a bewildered way. The
letters fell in little burning fragments about the hearth. It was
all like a terrible dream. He

watched those steady fingers hold
letter after letter in the candle
flame, and watched the candle
burning on like a passion in the
grey daylight of universal existence. A draught from under the
door began blowing the ash about
the room. The voice said—

"You tried to marry a rich
girl. You did not love her, but
knew she was rich. You tired
of her as you tire of so many
things, and behaved to her most
wrongly, most wickedly and
treacherously. When you were
jilted you came again to me and
to the idleness of this little town.
We had all hoped great things
of you. You seemed good and
honest."

"I loved you all along," he
cried. "If you would marry me
we would be very happy. I loved
you all along," he repeated—this
helplessly, several times over.
The bird shook a shower of seed
on his shoulder. He picked one
of them from the collar of his
coat and turned it over in his

fingers mechanically. "I loved you all along."

"You have done no duty that came to you. You have tired of everything you should cling to; and now you have come to this little town because here is idleness and irresponsibility."

The last letter lay in ashes on the hearth. She blew out the candle, and replaced it among the photographs on the mantlepiece, and stood there as calm as a portion of the marble.

"John, our friendship is over—it has been burnt in the candle."

He started forward, his mind full of appeals half-stifled with despair, on his lips gathered incoherent words: "She will be happy with Howard. They were made for each other. I slipped into it. I always thought I should marry some one who was rich. I never loved any one but you. I did not know I loved you at first. I thought about you always. You are the root of my life."

Steps were heard outside the door at the end of a passage. Mary Carton went to the door and called. The steps turned and came nearer. With a great effort Sherman controlled himself. The door opened, and a tall, slight girl of twelve came into the room. A strong smell of garden mould rose from a basket in her hands. Sherman recognized the child who had given him tea that evening in the schoolhouse three years before.

"Have you finished weeding the carrots?" said Mary Carton.

"Yes, Miss."

"Then you are to weed the small bed under the pear-tree by the tool-house. Do not go yet, child. This is Mr. Sherman. Sit down a little."

The child sat down on the corner of a chair with a scared look in her eyes. Suddenly she said—

"Oh, what a lot of burnt paper!"

"Yes; I have been burning some old letters."

"I think," said John, "I will go now." Without a word of farewell he went out, almost groping his way.

He had lost the best of all the things he held dear. Twice he had gone through the fire. The first time worldly ambition left him, on the second love. An hour before the air had been full of singing and peace that was resonant like joy. Now he saw standing before his Eden the angel with the flaming sword. All the hope he had ever gathered about him had taken itself off, and the naked soul shivered.

IV.

HE road under his feet felt gritty and barren. He hurried away from the town. It was late afternoon. Trees cast bands of shadow across the road. He walked rapidly as if pursued. About a mile to the south of the town he came on a large wood bordering the road and surrounding a deserted house. Some local rich man once lived there, now it was given over to a caretaker who lived in two rooms in the back part. Men were at work cutting down trees in two or three parts of the wood. Many places were quite bare. A mass of ruins—a covered well, and the wreckage of castle wall

—that had been roofed with green for centuries lifted themselves up, bare as anatomies. The sight intensified, by some strange sympathy, his sorrow, and he hurried away as from a thing accursed of God.

The road led to the foot of a mountain, topped by a cairn supposed in popular belief to be the grave of Maeve, Mab of the fairies, and considered by antiquarians to mark the place where certain prisoners were executed in legendary times as sacrifices to the moon.

He began to climb the mountain. The sun was on the rim of the sea. It stayed there without moving, for as he ascended he saw an ever-widening circle of water.

He threw himself down upon the cairn. The sun sank under the sea. The Donegal headlands mixed with the surrounding blue. The stars grew out of heaven.

Sometimes he got up and walked to and fro. Hours passed.

The stars, the streams down in the valley, the wind moving among the boulders, the various unknown creatures rustling in the silence—all these were contained within themselves, fulfilling their law, content to be alone, content to be with others, having the peace of God or the peace of the birds of prey. He only did not fulfil his law; something that was not he, that was not nature, that was not God, had made him and her he loved its tools. Hope, memory, tradition, conformity, had been laying waste their lives. As he thought this the night seemed to crush him with its purple foot. Hour followed hour. At midnight he started up, hearing a faint murmur of clocks striking the hour in the distant town. His face and hands were wet with tears, his clothes saturated with dew.

He turned homeward, hurriedly flying from the terrible firmament. What had this glimmering and silence to do with him—this luxu-

rious present? He belonged to
the past and the future. With
pace somewhat slackened, because
of the furze, he came down into
the valley. Along the northern
horizon moved a perpetual dawn,
travelling eastward as the night
advanced. Once, as he passed a
marsh near a lime-kiln, a number
of small birds rose chirruping
from where they had been cling-
ing among the reeds. Once,
standing still for a moment where
two roads crossed on a hill-side,
he looked out over the dark fields.
A white stone rose in the middle
of a field, a score of yards in
front of him. He knew the place
well; it was an ancient burying-
ground. He looked at the stone,
and suddenly filled by that terror
of the darkness children feel,
began again his hurried walk.

He re-entered Ballah by the
southern side. In passing he
looked at the rectory. To his
surprise a light burned in the
drawing-room. He stood still.
The dawn was brightening to-

wards the east, but all round him
was darkness, seeming the more
intense to his eyes for their being
fresh from the unshaded fields.
In the midst of this darkness
shone the lighted window. He
went over to the gate and looked
in. The room was empty. He
was about to turn away when he
noticed a white figure standing
close to the gate. The latch
creaked and the gate moved
slowly on its hinges.

" John," said a trembling voice,
"I have been praying, and a light
has come to me. I wished you
to be ambitious—to go away and
do something in the world. You
did badly, and my poor pride
was wounded. You do not know
how much I had hoped from you ;
but it was all pride—all pride and
foolishness. You love me. I ask
no more. We need each other ;
the rest is with God."

She took his hand in hers, and
began caressing it. "We have
been shipwrecked. Our goods
have been cast into the sea."

9

Something in her voice told of
the emotion that divides the love
of woman from the love of man.
She looked upon him whom she
loved as full of a helplessness
that needed protection, a rever-
beration of the feeling of the
mother for the child at the
breast.

DHOYA.

I.

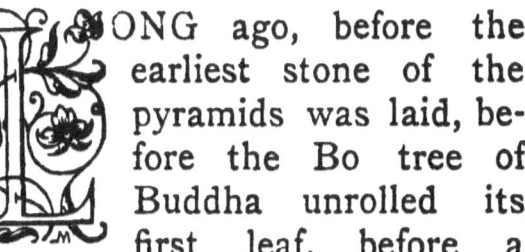ONG ago, before the earliest stone of the pyramids was laid, before the Bo tree of Buddha unrolled its first leaf, before a Japanese had painted on a temple wall the horse that every evening descended and trampled the rice-fields, before the ravens of Thor had eaten their first worm together, there lived a man of giant stature and of giant strength named Dhoya. One evening Fomorian galleys had entered the Bay of the Red Cataract, now the Bay of Ballah, and there deserted him. Though he rushed into the water and hurled great stones after them

they were out of reach. From
earliest childhood the Fomorians
had held him captive and compelled him to toil at the oar, but
when his strength had come his
fits of passion made him a terror
to all on board. Sometimes he
would tear the seats of the galley
from their places, at others drive
the rowers to some corner where,
trembling, they would watch him
pacing to and fro till the passion
left him. "The demons," they
said, "have made him their
own." So they enticed him on
shore, he having on his head a
mighty stone pitcher to fill with
water, and deserted him.

When the last sail had dropped
over the rim of the world he
rose from where he had flung
himself down on the sands and
paced through the forests eastward. After a time he reached
that lake among the mountains
where in later times Dermot
drove down four stakes and made
thereon a platform with four
flags in the centre for a hearth,

and placed over all a roof of
wicker and skins, and hid his
Grania, islanded thereon. Still
eastward he went, what is now
Bulban on one side, Cope's
mountain on the other, until at
last he threw himself at full
length in a deep cavern and
slept. Henceforward he made
this cavern his lair, issuing forth
to hunt the deer or the bears or
the mountain oxen. Slowly the
years went by, his fits of fury
growing more and more frequent,
though there was no one but his
own shadow to rave against.
When his fury was on him even
the bats and owls, and the brown
toads that crept out of the grass
at twilight would hide themselves—even the bats and owls
and the brown toads. These he
had made his friends, and let
them crawl and perch about
him, for at times he would be
very gentle, and they too were
sullen and silent—the outcasts
from they knew not what. But
most of all, things placid and

beautiful feared him. He would
watch for hours, hidden in the
leaves, to reach his hand out
slowly and carefully at last, and
seize and crush some glittering
halcyon.

Slowly the years went by and
human face he never saw, but
sometimes, when the gentle mood
was on him and it was twilight,
a presence seemed to float in-
visibly by him and sigh softly,
and once or twice he awoke from
sleep with the sensation of a
finger having rested for a moment on his forehead, and would
mutter a prayer to the moon
before turning to sleep again—
the moon that glimmered through
the door of his cave. "O
moon," he would say, "that
wandereth in the blue cave,
more white than the beard of
Partholan, whose years were five
hundred, sullen and solitary,
sleeping only on the floor of the
sea : keep me from the evil
spirits of the islands of the lake
southward beyond the mountains,

and the evil spirits of the caves
northward beyond the mountains, and the evil spirits who
wave their torches by the mouth
of the river eastward beyond the
valley, and the evil spirits of
the pools westward beyond the
mountains, and I will offer you a
bear and a deer in full horn, O
solitary of the cave divine, and if
any have done you wrong I will
avenge you."

Gradually, however, he began
to long for this mysterious touch.

At times he would make jour-
neys into distant parts, and once
the mountain oxen gathered together, proud of their over-
whelming numbers and their
white horns, and followed him
with great bellowing westward,
he being laden with their tallest,
well-nigh to his cave, and would
have gored him, but, pacing into
a pool of the sea to his shoulders,
he saw them thunder away,
losing him in the darkness. The
place where he stood is called
Pooldhoya to this day.

So the years went slowly by,
and ever deeper and deeper
came his moodiness, and more
often his fits of wrath. Once in
his gloom he paced the forests
for miles, now this way now that,
until, returning in the twilight, he
found himself standing on a cliff
southward of the lake that was
southward of the mountains.
The moon was rising. The
sound of the swaying of reeds
floated from beneath, and the
twittering of the flocks of reed-
wrens who love to cling on the
moving stems. It was the hour
of votaries. He turned to the
moon, then hurriedly gathered a
pile of leaves and branches, and
making a fire cast thereon wild
strawberries and the fruit of the
quicken tree. As the smoke
floated upwards a bar of faint
purple clouds drifted over the
moon's face—a refusal of the
sacrifice. Hurrying through the
surrounding woods he found an
owl sleeping in the hollow of a
tree, and returning cast him

on the fire. Still the clouds
gathered. Again he searched
the woods. This time a badger
was uselessly cast among the
flames. Time after time he came
and went, sometimes returning
immediately with some live thing,
at others not till the fire had
almost burnt itself out. Deer,
wild swine, birds, all to no purpose. Higher and higher he
piled the burning branches, the
flames and the smoke waved and
circled like the lash of a giant's
wbip. Gradually the nearer islands passed the rosy colour on
to their more distant brethren.
The reed-wrens of the furthest
reed beds disturbed amid their
sleep must have wondered at the
red gleam reflected in each
other's eyes. Useless his night-
long toil ; the clouds covered the
moon's face more and more,
until, when the long fire lash was
at its brightest, they drowned her
completely in a surge of unbroken
mist. Raging against the fire he
scattered with his staff the burn-

ing branches, and trampled in
his fury the sacrificial embers
beneath his feet. Suddenly a
voice in the surrounding darkness called him softly by name.
He turned. For years no articu-
late voice had sounded in his
ears. It seemed to rise from the
air just beneath the verge of the
precipice. Holding by a hazel
bush he leaned out, and for a
moment it seemed to him the
form of a beautiful woman floated
faintly before him, but changed
as he watched to a little cloud of
vapour ; and from the nearest of
the haunted islands there came
assuredly a whiff of music. Then
behind him in the forest said the
voice, " Dhoya, my beloved."
He rushed in pursuit; something
white was moving before him.
He stretched out his hand ; it
was only a mass of white campion
trembling in the morning breeze,
for an ashen morning was just
touching the mists on the eastern
mountains. Beginning suddenly
to tremble with supernatural

fear Dhoya paced homewards.
Everything was changed ; dark
shadows seemed to come and go,
and elfin chatter to pass upon
the breeze. But when he reached
the shelter of the pine woods all
was still as of old. He slackened
his speed. Those solemn pine-
trees soothed him with their vast
unsociability—many and yet each
one alone. Once or twice, when
in some glade further than usual
from its kind arose some pine-
tree larger than the rest, he
paused with bowed head to
mutter an uncouth prayer to
that dark outlaw. But when
issuing once more, as he neared
his cave, into the region of mountain ash and hazel the voices
seemed again to come and go,
and the shadows to circle round
him, and once a voice said, he
imagined, in accents faint and
soft as falling dew, " Dhoya, my
beloved." But a few yards from
the cave all grew suddenly silent.

II.

SLOWER and slower he went, with his eyes on the ground, bewildered by all that was happening. A few feet from the cave he stood still, counting aimlessly the round spots of light made by the beams slanting through trees that hid with their greenness, as in the centre of the sea, that hollow rock. As over and over he counted them, he heard, first with the ear only, then with the mind also, a footstep going to and fro within the cave. Lifting his eyes he saw the same figure seen on the cliff —the figure of a woman, beautiful and young. Her dress was white, save for a border of

feathers dyed the fatal red of
the spirits. She had arranged
in one corner the spears, and in
the other the brushwood and
branches used for the fire, and
spread upon the ground the skins,
and now began pulling vainly
at the great stone pitcher of the
Fomorians.

Suddenly she saw him, and
with a burst of wild laughter
flung her arms around his neck,
crying, " Dhoya, I have left my
world far off. My people—on
the floor of the lake they are
dancing and singing, and on the
islands of the lake ; always
happy, always young, always
without change. I have left
them for thee, Dhoya, for they
cannot love. Only the changing,
and moody, and angry, and
weary can love. I am beautiful ;
love me, Dhoya. Do you hear
me ? I left the places where
they dance, Dhoya, for thee ! "
For long she poured out a tide of
words, he answering at first
little, then more and more as she

melted away the silence of so
many inarticulate years; and all
the while she gazed on him with
eyes, no ardour could rob of the
mild and mysterious melancholy
that watches us from the eyes
of animals—sign of unhuman
reveries.

Many days passed over these
strangely wedded ones. Sometimes when he asked her, " Do
you love me ? " she would answer,
" I do not know, but I long for
your love endlessly." Often at
twilight, returning from hunting,
he would find her bending over a
stream that flowed near to the
cave, decking her hair with
feathers and reddening her lips
with the juice of a wild berry.

He was very happy secluded
in that deep forest. Hearing the
faint murmurs of the western
sea, they seemed to have outlived
change. But Change is everywhere, with the tides and the stars
fastened to her wheel. Every
blood drop in their lips, every
cloud in the sky, every leaf in

the world changed a little, while
they brushed back their hair and
kissed. All things change save
only the fear of change. And
yet for his hour Dhoya was
happy and as full of dreams as
an old man or an infant—for
dreams wander nearest to the
grave and the cradle.

Once, as he was returning home
from hunting, by the northern
edge of the lake, at the hour
when the owls cry to each other,
"It is time to be abroad," and
the last flutter of the wind has
died away, leaving under every
haunted island an image legible
to the least hazel branch, there
suddenly stood before him a
slight figure, at the edge of the
narrow sand-line, dark against
the glowing water. Dhoya drew
nearer. It was a man leaning
on his spear-staff, on his head a
small red cap. His spear was
slender and tipped with shining
metal ; the spear of Dhoya of
wood, one end pointed and har-
dened in the fire. The red-

capped stranger silently raised
that slender spear and thrust at
Dhoya, who parried with his
pointed staff.

For a long while they fought.
The last vestige of sunset passed
away and the stars came out.
Underneath them the feet of
Dhoya beat up the ground, but
the feet of the other as he rushed
hither and thither, matching his
agility with the mortal's mighty
strength, made neither shadow
nor footstep on the sands.
Dhoya was wounded, and growing weary a little, when the other
leaped away, and, crouching down
by the water, began—" You have
carried away by some spell unknown the most beautiful of our
bands—you who have neither
laughter nor singing. Restore
her, Dhoya, and go free." Dhoya
answered him no word, and the
other rose and again thrust at
him with the spear. They fought
to and fro upon the sands until
the dawn touched with olive the
distant sky, and then his anger

fit, long absent, fell on Dhoya,
and he closed with his enemy
and threw him, and put his knee
on his chest and his hands on
his throat, and would have
crushed all life out of him, when
lo ! he held beneath his knee no
more than a bundle of reeds.

Nearing home in the early
morning he heard the voice he
loved, singing—

" Full moody is my love and sad,
   His moods bow low his sombre crest,
I hold him dearer than the glad,
   And he shall slumber on my breast.

" My love hath many an evil mood
   Ill words for all things soft and fair,
I hold him dearer than the good,
   My fingers feel his amber hair.

" No tender wisdom floods the eyes
   That watch me with their suppliant
      light—
I hold him dearer than the wise,
   And for him make me wise and
      bright."

And when she saw him she cried,
" An old mortal song heard
floating from a tent of skin, as

we rode, I and mine, through a
camping-place at night." From
that day she was always either
singing wild and melancholy
songs or else watching him with
that gaze of animal reverie.

Once he asked, " How old are
you ? "

" A thousand years, for I am
young."

" I am so little to you," he
went on, " and you are so much
to me—dawn, and sunset, tran-
quility, and speech, and solitude."

" Am I so much ? " she said ;
" say it many times ! " and her
eyes seemed to brighten and her
breast heaved with joy.

Often he would bring her the
beautiful skins of animals, and
she would walk to and fro on
them, laughing to feel their soft-
ness under her feet. Sometimes
she would pause and ask suddenly, " Will you weep for me
when we have parted ? " and he
would answer, " I will die then ; "
and she would go on rubbing her
feet to and fro in the soft skin.

And so Dhoya grew tranquil
and gentle, and Change seemed
still to have forgotten them,
having so much on her hands.
The stars rose and set watching
them smiling together, and the
tides ebbed and flowed, bringing
mutability to all save them. But
always everything changes, save
only the fear of Change.

III.

ONE evening as they sat in the inner portion of the cave, watching through the opening the paling of the sky and the darkening of the leaves, and counting the budding stars, Dhoya suddenly saw stand before him the dark outline of him he fought on the lake sand, and heard at the same instant his companion sigh.

The stranger approached a little, and said, " Dhoya we have fought heretofore, and now I have come to play chess against thee, for well thou knowest, dear to the perfect warrior after war is chess."

" I know it," answered Dhoya.

"And when we have played,
Dhoya, we will name the stake."
"Do not play," whispered his
companion at his side.

But Dhoya, being filled with
his anger fit at the sight of his
enemy, answered, "I will play,
and I know well the stake you
mean, and I name this for mine,
that I may again have my knee
on your chest and my hands on
your throat, and that you will
not again change into a bundle
of wet reeds." His companion
lay down on a skin and began to
cry a little.

Dhoya felt sure of winning. He
had often played in his boyhood,
before the time of his anger fits,
with his masters of the galley;
and besides, he could always
return to his hands and his
weapons once more.

Now the floor of the cave was
of smooth, white sand, brought
from the sea-shore in his great
Fomorian pitcher, to make it
soft for his beloved to walk upon;
before it had been, as it now is,

of rough clay. On this sand the
red-capped stranger marked out
with his spear-point a chess-
board, and marked with rushes,
crossed and recrossed each
alternate square, fixing each end
of the rush in the sand, until a
complete board was finished of
white and green squares, and then
drew from a bag large chess-men
of mingled wood and silver. Two
or three would have made an
armful for a child. Standing
each at his end they began to
play. The game did not last
long. No matter how carefully
Dhoya played, each move went
against him. At last, leaping
back from the board he cried, " I
have lost ! " The two spirits
were standing together at the
entrance. Dhoya seized his
spear, but slowly the figures
began to fade, first a star and
then the leaves showed through
their forms. Soon all had
vanished away.

Then, realizing his loss, he
threw himself on the ground,

and rolling hither and thither,
roared like a wild beast. All
night long he lay on the ground,
and all the next day till nightfall. He had crumbled his staff
unconsciously between his fingers
into small pieces, and now, full
of dull rage, arose and went forth
westward. In a ravine of the
northern mountain he came on
the tracks of wild horses. Soon
one passed him fearlessly, knowing nothing of man. The pointed
end of his staff he still carried.
He drove it deep in the flank,
making a long wound, sending
the horse rushing with short
screams down the mountain.
Other horses passed him one by
one, driven southward by a cold
wind laden with mist, arisen in
the night-time. Towards the
end of the ravine stood one black
and huge, the leader of the herd.
Dhoya leaped on his back with
a loud cry that sent a raven
circling from the neighbouring
cliff, and the horse, after vainly
seeking to throw him, rushed off

towards the north-west, over the
heights of the mountains where
the mists floated. The moon,
clear sometimes of the flying
clouds, from low down in the
south-east, cast a pale and mu-
table light, making their shadow
rise before them on the mists,
as though they pursued some
colossal demon, sombre on his
black charger. Then leaving
the heights they rushed wildly
down that valley where, in far
later times, Dermot hid in a
deep cavern his Grania, and
passed the stream where Muad-
han, their savage servant, caught
fish for them on a hook baited
with a quicken berry. On over
the plains, on northward, mile
after mile, the wild gigantic horse
leaping cliff and chasm in his
terrible race; on until the mountains of what is now Donegal
rose before them—over these
among the clouds, driving rain
blowing in their faces from the
sea, Dhoya knowing not whither
he went, or why he rode. On—

the stones loosened by the hoofs
rumbling down into the valleys
—till far in the distance he saw
the sea, a thousand feet below
him; then, fixing his eyes thereon,
and using the spear-point as a
goad, he roused his black horse
into redoubled speed, and with a
wild leap horse and rider plunged
headlong into the Western Sea.

Sometimes the cotters on the
mountains of Donegal hear on
windy nights a sudden sound of
horses' hoofs, and say to each
other, " There goes Dhoya."
And at the same hour men say
if any be abroad in the valleys
they see a huge shadow rushing
along the mountain.

THE END.

𝕿𝖍𝖊 𝕲𝖗𝖊𝖘𝖍𝖆𝖒 𝕻𝖗𝖊𝖘𝖘,

UNWIN BROTHERS

CHILWORTH AND LONDON.

www.ingramcontent.com/pod-product-compliance
Lightning Source LLC
Chambersburg PA
CBHW030124030726